LANDING HER EAGLE

SHIFTING PINES
BOOK ONE

JENNY FENSHAW

SHIFTING PINES PRESS

1

DAPHNE

"Good afternoon. Morgan Development, Daphne Foster speaking. How may I help you?"

Ugh. Why do Mondays come so soon? Obviously, there are people who enjoy their jobs and look forward to working, but that's not me. There's nothing wrong with my job. I help manage a handful of homeowners' associations in Shifting Pines, New Jersey. I'm paid well, I like the people I work with. It's not difficult. This job is like that boy who asks you out on a date. You go because he's nice and you like him, but you don't like-like him. There's no spark. You feel guilty. You know he's a catch and many girls would love to date him. You feel like there's something wrong with you for not feeling it. There isn't, of course. You either have chemistry or you don't, and that's fine. You want there to be a spark, but all you have is a fizzled sparkler.

Lately, I've been feeling like my whole life is a fizzled sparkler. I spend all week at a job that offers security but no stimulation. Once in a while someone doesn't pay their association dues or puts more than two plastic flamingos in their yard and the attorney I work with needs to send a letter I type telling them to knock it the flock off. This past weekend, like all those before, I sat at home watching reruns of *Murder, She Wrote* while knitting. Jessica Fletcher has traveled the world, adventuring well into her sixties. I spend my weekends sitting on my couch surrounded by yarn.

I'm too young to be this old.

I listen to the lady on the phone complain about a letter she received from our office and recommend that she email the attorney listed to work out a solution to her situation. Eight more minutes, and then I can go home and get ready to enjoy the best part of my week. I can do this.

As soon as my computer clock says five o'clock, I exit out of all the programs and shut down my computer. I walk out of the building with my coworker.

"Night, Mallory!" I wave as I duck into my car.

Since I didn't leave the house all weekend, I need to swing by the supermarket on my way home so I have food for the week. I'm annoyed with myself for putting it off again, but I didn't feel like shopping Friday, and I was really comfy on my couch all weekend.

I should sign up for one of those food delivery companies that sends you everything you need to cook a meal. A box on my doorstep every week would be so much better than the hell on Earth that is the supermarket. Everyone is buying their groceries tonight. Apparently, no one has used a self-check lane before and wants to give it a try tonight. I want to offer my skills gained as a cashier from my high school job and check them out just to get them gone, but I'm not allowed to do that anymore after last time. Whatever. Their loss.

The frustration continues in the car on the way home. "Go!" I scream at the car in front of me. Who stops for a yellow light in New Jersey? Now I'm stuck here for at least another cycle. Finally, I get through the light and drive as quickly as legally possible. With a sigh of relief, I pull into the driveway of my ranch home. Grabbing my bags and hurrying inside, I grumble because I hate having to rush. I check the grandfather clock in the living room corner. It's almost seven o'clock. Usually, I wish the seconds would tick by faster, but tonight I need an extra moment to get myself together. I've just settled in with my iPad, phone, and rum with a splash of Diet Pepsi when my iPad dings. I smile when Logan's face appears, wanting to FaceTime.

Yay! I love it when I can see him while we talk.

Yes, he is gorgeous with his wavy dark brown hair and forest-green eyes, but what really makes him so attractive are his facial expressions and the way he focuses on the person he's speaking with. He can say more with a quirked brow than most people say in five minutes of uninterrupted babbling. When he's talking to you, you feel you're the center of his universe, like no one else exists to him but you.

I can't suppress my giggle as the screen comes to life with my favorite face. "Hey, you! Where are you this week?"

Logan smiles. "Hey, Daph! I'm in Prague. You'd love it here. It's gorgeous. The Baroque architecture is incredible. I can't wait to show you the shots I've taken."

Logan is a travel photographer focusing on European cities and architecture. We met in a history and architecture class our sopho-more year of college and have been best friends ever since. He was a business major headed to law school, and I was an accounting major. We were each following in our parents' footsteps. Instead of law school, he discovered his love of—and talent for—photography. I don't know if it's that he's a golden eagle shifter and gets a literal bird's-eye view of things that makes him so skilled, or if he possesses an innate talent, but his work is incredible.

"I bet they are stunning, like always. I can't wait to see them. Where do you go next?" My lips curve into a loving smile.

"I don't know where I'm headed next, but you're welcome to come along."

My heart leaps. He's so considerate, always inviting me on his adventures. He's a good friend, but I wish he saw me as more. Maybe it's because I can't shift? What fun would it be to be stuck with someone landbound when you're able to soar high? I guess I'd be handy to watch the bags.

"Thanks," I respond, "but some of us have a Monday-through-Friday, nine-to-five life to live."

"That you hate," he retorts. "I don't understand why you trap yourself in an office. Gran told me how you used to dream of traveling. Remember that? You were going to be a tour guide?" A flurry of unspoken, frustrated emotions flash across his face.

I recognize them because I feel them in my chest too. I take a deep breath to quiet them.

"You know I can't leave this house. I don't want to be gone months at a time."

"Get someone to watch it for you. Rent it out."

It's so easy for him to make suggestions like that. He hasn't lost what I have. He doesn't understand my need to have a safe harbor. It wasn't always like this. When I was younger, I craved travel and adventure. I covered my walls with maps and calendar pictures of far-off places.

Then my parents died, and I started isolating myself. In a flash of headlights, I lost my world. I was in high school when the accident happened, and I moved in with Gran. She passed away while I was in college, so now this house is all I have left of my family.

I can't lose it too.

Logan is always leaving. Everyone leaves me.

Gah, I sound so whiny and pathetic. People leave because I insist on staying put. Whatever. This house isn't leaving me, and I don't want to leave it.

2

LOGAN

I CAN SEE THE LONGING AND FUTILITY IN DAPHNE'S FACE EVEN THROUGH A screen and over six thousand miles. I don't need to be on the same continent as her to know she wants what she's always wanted—excitement, travel, adventure—but that she'll never take it for herself.

I want to take a screenshot so she sees what I do and convince her to do something about it, but she'll shut down and find a reason to end our call. It hurts me to see her sad, but it would hurt me more not to see her at all. Better to change the conversation.

"So, what did you do over the weekend?"

I have a feeling what the answer will be, but maybe she'll surprise me.

"The usual. I read a new book by my favorite author, ordered yarn for a shawl pattern I've been wanting to try, and there was a *Murder, She Wrote* marathon."

I hold her gaze with mine. "You know you're twenty-six, not eighty-six, right? You—"

She huffs and turns away from the screen. She doesn't want to hear what I have to say, but I'm going to say it anyway.

"You should be out at a club dancing with your girlfriends, not sitting at home, knitting and watching shows that were off the air before you started kindergarten," I say.

Daphne sips her drink and shoots me a pointed glare. "First of all, you know I'm a horrible dancer. Second, my best friend is gallivanting all over Europe, and Shelby is all loved up with her new Bigfoot shifter boyfriend, so I have no one to go to the club with." She hiccups and takes another sip. "Fourth of all, shut up. J.B. Fletcher is awesome."

I narrow my gaze at Daphne. "How many of those"—I motion with my chin toward her glass of what I presume is rum and Diet Pepsi—"have you had tonight?"

She flushes a light pink. "Just one."

I snort. "You know I'm aware of your trick of not taking the last sip and refilling so you can say you've only had one when it's more like three or four."

"Of course you know it! You taught me that trick!"

Shrugging, I can't help the smirk that forms on my lips.

"You are a lousy liar. The trick helps you avoid it."

Daphne sticks her tongue out at me.

"You can't be mad at me for learning my lessons well! Anyway." She pauses dramatically. "I'm going on an adventure next weekend!"

Even on the dimly lit, blurry screen, she sparkles. She's vibrating with energy, bouncing up and down in her seat, her smile stretching wider than I've seen it in years. Her brown eyes are shining in a way I don't see often enough, and she pushes her dark brown ponytail over her shoulder. When she bounces happily in her seat, her boobs jiggle. I like that very much. She may solely think of me as her best friend, but she's my everything.

My heart constricts to see her so happy, so excited. Other parts expand, and I shift in my seat to ease the pressure in my jeans.

"That's awesome! Where are you going? What are you doing?"

"It's the New Jersey Lighthouse Challenge weekend, and I'm going to do it. Have you heard of it? It's the third weekend of October, and it's a self-guided driving tour of the land-based lighthouses in New Jersey. If you do the whole thing, you cover the Atlantic coast, the Delaware Bay coastline, and a bit of the Delaware River. There is so much history and unique architecture with great scenery on the drive. My parents and I used to do it every year."

Her bright gaze falters, her light dimming. It could be the screen resolution or a bad bit of Wi-Fi, but it isn't. She misses her parents.

She shakes it off, and her face lights up again.

"Saturday morning, I'll start at Sandy Hook and do the Atlantic coast lighthouses, ending at the Absecon Lighthouse in Atlantic City. Sunday, I'll start over in Paulsboro and do the river and bay lighthouses and finish at Cape May, like we always did."

I swallow, my throat tight. I'm thrilled she's going out and doing this. I never met her parents, but when she speaks of them, you can hear the love in her voice and see the sorrow in her expression. Looking at pictures, you can see how close they were. It's not fair that they left her alone because of a drunk driver's thoughtless actions.

"Anyway," she continues, "I'll finish at the Cape May Lighthouse. Depending on the time, maybe I'll go to Sunset Beach and search for Cape May diamonds. Since there's no romance at the lighthouse in my future, I'll get my own diamond." She laughs.

This is new. I love seeing her happy; that's what I want for her. But she's finally going on an adventure, and I'm not there to share it with her. She's only ever talked about them in the abstract before. She's never actually planned anything.

What else is she planning? Is she going to go out, start dating? Is she going to find someone? Guys have been trying to get her attention for years, but she never notices. What if she notices now? I'm across the Atlantic from her. She won't be thinking of me when she has someone right in front of her. Why is she changing now? Is she finally making the change I've been dreaming of?

Daphne clears her throat, refocusing my attention.

"I'm sorry. What?"

She rolls her eyes and sways a bit. Her "one drink" is starting to hit her. "How long are you in Prague?"

I think about how to answer, my mind running through a few scenarios.

"I'm not sure. Another week or two. Listen, Daph, I need to edit some pictures. I don't know if I'll be able to FaceTime more this week, but I'll text you. Promise me you'll do the lighthouse challenge. I know when it comes time to get in the car and go, you'll make excuses to stay home. Promise me."

She gives a half smile. "Gee, a girl doesn't leave her house for weeks at a time except to go to work, and people think she's a hermit or something. I promise."

"Good. To hold you to it, take a selfie at each lighthouse and text it to me while you're there."

"Really, Logan Morris? You need proof? Do you want me to hold up a newspaper too, to prove the date?" She sounds exasperated, but she wears a playful smirk.

"Nah, a selfie will do the trick." I wink. "Have a good...okay, not sucky...week at work. Drive safely and have fun next weekend. Remember—selfies and texts."

"Goodnight, Logan. Have fun, be safe, take pretty pictures." She smiles, waves, and disconnects.

My phone dings, signaling a text. I smile as I pick it up, expecting it to be Daphne with something she forgot to say.

It's not. It's my cousin, Liam.

> Liam: I saw your girl today.

> Me: Daphne?

> Liam: Do you have some other girl?

> Me: No.

> Liam: Are you guys dating?

How do I answer him? We aren't dating, but my goal is to change that. Eventually. Maybe sooner than eventually if Daphne's light-house adventure is a sign of bigger changes to come, a sign she's *ready*. Finally.

> Liam: Because if you aren't, I'm going to ask her out.

> Me: NO!

> Liam: No, you aren't dating?

> Me: WTF dude, leave her alone.

> Liam: Dude, if you don't ask her out, I will. She's too cute to be single.

> Me: Don't make me kick your ass.

> Liam: I know you're all shifter strong and shit, but you'd have to get your eagle self here to kick my ass. You aren't doing anything from across the ocean.

What. The. Hell? Other than Daphne, Liam is my best friend. Why is he doing this? He's only a year older than I am, and we did everything together growing up. He works for the same company Daphne does, traveling around the country, scouting new locations for Morgan Outlet Centers and visiting existing centers making sure they're running smoothly. I don't know how he thinks he's going to date Daphne when he's not home much more than I am!

I end our text conversation with the middle finger emoji and start Googling flights back home. While my relationship with Daphne started as a friendship, through the years, my feelings for her have deepened. I would love to pursue something with her, but I'm so firmly established in the friend zone, I've considered having my mail forwarded there. Part of the reason I travel so much is that it kills me to be close to Daphne and just be her friend. If I was close to her, I'd want more, and she hasn't been ready for that. If she'd even want me that way. Maybe it's all one-sided on my part.

My eagle knows she's the one for me. Sure, I've dated. I haven't been a monk since I met her, but those shallow encounters haven't dulled the knowledge that she's the one I'm meant to share my life with.

What if she doesn't think I'm who she's supposed to share her life with? Maybe she doesn't want to marry a shifter. At least that would rule out Liam. He's a cougar shifter, like my mom and brother. Like his dad and sister too. Sure, we'll play the field some when we're young and single shifters, but when we commit to a mate, it's for life. I can't have a fling with her—if we do this, it's forever. Maybe she doesn't consider me forever material? I guess I'm going to have to man up and find out.

If she's ready for an adventure, I'm going to be the one to give it to her.

3

FROM THE TEXTS OF LOGAN AND DAPHNE

Logan: Hey. Happy Wednesday. How's work?

Daphne: Same as always.

Logan: I'm sorry. Anyway. Still doing your lighthouse thing this weekend?

Daphne: Yeah. Still in Prague? When will you be home next?

Logan: Still here. Figuring out what's next. Not sure about home.

Daphne: Hire me to be your virtual assistant. I could organize everything for you, that way you wouldn't have to research and plan things. I could work from home.

Logan: Or you could come with me, be my in-person assistant, and arrange everything to make my life easier.

Daphne: But then I wouldn't be home. I'd have to wear clothes.

Logan: Don't feel you have to on my account. I could do a series on nude beaches. I'm that good of a friend.

Daphne: WOW, the sacrifices you'll make in the name of friendship. :winky face emoji:

Logan: For you, anything. So, are you naked now? :smiley face emoji:

Daphne: What?! Don't be gross, Logan.

Logan: You started it.

Daphne: I did not!

Logan: You said you weren't wearing any clothes.

Daphne: No, I said I'd have to wear clothes since I wouldn't be at home.

Logan: Exactly. Since you ARE home, we can then surmise you are sans apparel.

Daphne:...

Logan: So, what are you wearing? :smiley face emoji:

Daphne:...

Logan: Come on, send me a picture.

Daphne: Lol, no!

Logan: What????? I'm not asking for nudes (however, you're welcome to send some anytime). Snap a picture how you are right now. I miss you.

Logan: The puppy dog picture is for puppy dog eyes.

Daphne: Gee, really? I thought you were going to hump my leg. :eye roll emoji:

Logan: I'm up for that.

Daphne: Eww… Creep.

Logan: I'm teasing, don't be such a dud.

FIVE MINUTES PASS.

Logan: Daphne?

FIVE MINUTES MORE PASS.

Logan: Daph? C'mon. I'm sorry. I was teasing. Please talk to me.

Daphne: I know. I'm used to you being a perv. I wanted to take a picture.

Logan: You took one? Show me!

Daphne: Ta-da! :clown picture:

Logan: Ack! Creepy clown pictures are not cool. You owe me an actual picture.

Daphne: Here you go. I showed you mine. Now show me yours.

4

LOGAN

I STARE AT DAPHNE'S PICTURE. IT'S A SELFIE SHOWING HER FACE AND UPPER body. I can see the quilt her gran made her in the background, so she's in her bedroom, sitting in that armchair she insisted I help her drag back to her apartment when we were in college. She was confident she could reupholster it and, after many trips to the fabric store and hours of forcing me to watch YouTube videos with her, she did it. She picked the dark green checked pattern I liked the most, saying the green reminded her of my eyes. She's pulled her dark brown curls up in a clip atop her head, with a few escaping to caress the side of her neck. Long, dark lashes frame her sparkling brown eyes. Her lips. Man, her lips are full and tipped up in a sweet smile. Her lips are a bit sparkly.

> Me: I like your lipstick.

> Daphne: Thanks. My friend Andie recommended it. It feels weird to have something on my lips.

I imagine having my lips on her lips. Are they soft like they appear? Is that lipstick kiss-proof? How would it feel smeared across my mouth after kissing it off her? On other parts of me? I groan and start typing my reply.

> Me: Very nice. Make sure you wear it this weekend for your selfies at the lighthouses.

She's wearing a Hamilton University Rugby Club T-shirt. MY T-shirt. It's ridiculous, but I'm jealous that the cotton is caressing the curves I long to touch.

> Me: You're in another one of my shirts! You have a closet full of clothes and you keep stealing mine. I'm going to end up traveling topless!

> Daphne: And I'll get thank-you notes from ladies and guys the world over. This shirt is from school! You haven't worn it in like seven years!

> Me: Because you've had it!

> Daphne: Whatever. The fact of the matter is, it won't fit you. You've gotten all... muscly since then.

Well, well, well. She's noticed. About time.

> Daphne: I've shown you me, show me you.

I snap the pic and text it to Daphne. It's late, so I'm already in bed. I get comfy on the soft, white sheets while I wait for a response that doesn't come. I wake the next morning with my phone resting on my face and disappointment in my heart.

5

DAPHNE

"Wowsers," I whisper. I'm surprised my phone didn't spontaneously combust from Logan's picture. Damn, he's fine. He was texting from bed, and his chest was bare.

"The man should never wear shirts. It would be a crime to cover something so glorious." I steal his shirts as a public service, not because I miss him and can pretend he's holding me while I sleep.

Soooo many muscles. Is it physically possible he has a twelve-pack of abs? His muscles have muscles. Shifters are typically more muscular and agile than regular humans, and wow, his shifter genes are glorious things. No regular human would get so ripped taking pictures. I've never seen him in eagle form, but I'm sure he's gorgeous when he's shifted too. I know I'm not ugly, but I'm just *normal.* Why would someone so extraordinary want someone like me for anything other than friendship? Oh, that's right—he doesn't.

White sheets pool around his waist. He has a light dusting of hair on his pecs, and his brown happy trail disappears below the sheet. I try to scroll to see more, but the picture stops right below the sheet's edge. Darn.

He has his left arm tucked behind his head and his right arm extended to hold his phone up to take the snap. He's smiling, and his dark brown hair looks like a lover's fingers tousled it. Does he have a lover? We never discuss that sort of thing. It's not like we can swap stories. I have nothing to tell. The few dates I went on in high school and college were nothing serious. Nothing more than a couple of chaste kisses and sometimes not even that. I'm not sexy. I'm the girl next door. I'm the buddy. The pal. Whatever.

Logan is sexy, though. I bet he has women hitting on him all the time. Does he take them up on it? What's his type? Does he only go for shifter girls, or does he date humans too? He dated in college, but they were flings, not relationships. He wasn't a man-whore, but I'm sure he wasn't a monk either. He kept his extracurricular activities separate from our friendship.

I love being his friend, but I wish he saw me as a woman. I always thought Logan was attractive, but as I got to know him better in college, I developed stronger feelings for him— feelings I never expressed. It would freak him out. He'd pull away. I'd be lost without his friendship. He's my person. I would love the whole hearts and flowers experience, but if what we have now is all that I can have with him, I guess I'll settle for it.

But settling means I'll never know what he's like as a lover. I shift in my armchair, uncomfortable and, if I'm being honest, aroused. He's probably strong and masterful in bed. But not too rough. I don't want to stereotype him because he's a shifter, but sue me. I'm curious. He'd know how to touch a woman to make her feel good. I imagine his hands on my body and shiver. I run my hands over my breasts, wishing they were Logan's. My nipples harden. I've never had a man's mouth on my breasts, felt the rasp of his tongue around my areola. A tongue anywhere. I want that. I want so much. With Logan.

There's a throb between my legs. It's time to go to bed for some quality time with BOB, my battery-operated boyfriend. Hope I have batteries.

6

LOGAN

Daphne never responded to my picture. I hope I didn't offend her with my teasing. She rarely gets offended by sexual innuendo and is often the first to make an innocent comment dirty with a "That's what she said." It's one thing I love about her.

I'm packing up my gear for my trip. I guess I'll shoot her a text now since I'll be out of touch soon.

> Me: Hey, got a minute?

> Daphne: Hi. Yeah, driving to work. Using voice to text so anything weird is the car's fault. I'm not suddenly incontinent.

Let's assume she meant illiterate.

> Me: I may be hard to reach for a couple days, so wanted to check in and wish you a wonderful time this weekend.

> Daphne: Where are you going?

Me: Checking out things and doing a lot of editing. You know how I lose track of time.

Daphne: Oh. Okay. When are you leaving Prague?

Me: Soon.

Daphne: Where are you going Nexium?

Me: Next? Not sure. Still figuring things out.

Daphne: See, you need me. I'd have everything planned for you. You'd just have to show up. I can turn around and go home now and start planning.

Me: Lol, you truly don't want to go to work, do you?

Daphne: Nope.

Me: So do something else.

Daphne: I'm thinking about it.

My brows lift. Daphne hates change, so for her to even be thinking about it is a big deal.

Daphne: I'm pulling in. Now to go waste eight hours. I need a blow job. Have a good one.

Me: Me too. Bye.

Somewhere in my brain, I notice what I just wrote, but louder alarm bells are ringing out all over, and I'm trying not to panic.

She's ready for a change. Finally. And I'm not there. If she jumps when I'm not around, some other guy may catch her. Liam might catch her. And never let her go.

7

DAPHNE

I glance at the text conversation we had while I walk in. Awesome. My car does autocorrect on crack too. Incontinent? Nexium? I need a blow job? New job! I need a new job!

But his reply...Me too?! He needs a blow job?

Or did he know I meant a new job, and he's me too-ing that? Why would he want a new job? His job is incredible. He gets to go to so many places and have new experiences.

"You could have them too, if you'd stop being a wuss and go with him," I mutter to myself. Ugh. I need to get to my desk. I hope this isn't a very Monday-like Friday.

It is. It is the Monday-est Friday ever.

"Damn it!" The scanner chews up the documents I need to email to a client who is bugging me for them. My coworker, Mallory, took the day off so my misery has no company. I open the doors, following the copier instructions on the screen, my frustration mounting as I go through each step.

I slam the door after completing Step E when I hear a deep voice behind me. "Easy, Daph. What did this copy machine ever do to you?"

Glancing over my shoulder, I see Liam, Logan's cousin. "Hey, Liam, what are you doing here?"

Putting his hands on my shoulders and easing me aside, he says, "Move out of the way, and let me help so you don't assault the office equipment." He sweet-talks the copier. I swear he tells it what a wonderful machine it is and how hard it works and he's sorry it's not appreciated. He calls it Gabrielle, no lie.

"So, what are you doing here? I thought you were in Colorado or Arizona, checking out the outlets there. Are there hidden cameras I should pretend to not be aware of?"

"No, no cameras. I'm not doing an 'undercover boss' type of thing." He fiddles with a knob. "I'm not here to spy. I'm home for a couple of days and am taking care of some maintenance things in the office. No reason to call the management company when I can change lightbulbs myself. Your area needs a revamp."

Nodding enthusiastically, I plead, "Please tell me technology is getting an upgrade! What we have is functional, but I feel like down here is where the tech and furniture comes to die. It's fine getting cast-offs from upstairs, but I would love to edit a pdf without using an electric typewriter and Wite-Out."

"Wow." He laughs. "That's old school!"

"I know! It's crazy." I successfully run my document through the scanner. "Well, this was fun, but I have to send this."

He follows me and leans against Mallory's desk. "Is Logan in town?"

"He's in Prague. I'm not sure where he's going next."

"Are you two dating yet?"

I sigh. I'm so tired of this question. "We're friends."

He grins. "Do you have plans for this weekend?"

A blush rises in my cheeks. Liam is a flirt. He was flirting with the copier five minutes ago! But it's nice to have the attention. If I wasn't so hung up on Logan, I could easily crush on Liam. My head says Liam is the safe choice. He's here more than Logan. He doesn't tie my emotions into knots like Logan does. Liam travels for his job too, but I don't worry like I do when Logan is gone.

But my heart belongs to Logan, and if anything happened between me and Liam, that would end any hope of romance with Logan—and possibly our friendship too.

"I'm running errands," I say too quickly, hoping to hide my embarrassment. "What about you?"

"I'm going to the hockey game Saturday and meeting friends at Devil's Den tonight. You want to come along? Either? Both?"

"Nope, but thanks. And thank you for rescuing me from temperamental office equipment."

"Glad I was here to help. Seriously, call me if you want to hang out or if you ever give up on him."

Liam and Logan are close friends and cousins, but they're competitive too. I'm not a prize to be won.

"Are you around for the rest of the afternoon?" I ask.

"Nope. I'm checking out a property in Atlantic City. I'm going to head out now. Take care."

After he leaves, I sit down to work on filing for the rest of the afternoon. That's mindless. I need mindless.

Ooh, bonus, I got tedious and frustrating too. Yay. Nothing makes a Friday more fun than playing 52 Card Pickup with the huge paper stack you had meticulously put in alphabetical order so you could get some much-needed filing done. We won't mention the paper cut I got from the file jacket. I swear, my pinky needed a tourniquet to stop the bleeding.

"Home sweet home," I moan as I let myself into the house after work. Flopping onto the sofa, I decide I'm going to meld with it, become one with it. At least for the weekend. No reason to leave the house until work on Monday, right? The lighthouses aren't going anywhere. They've been there over a hundred years already. No rush. I can do the challenge next year. Yeah, good plan.

My phone signals a new text.

> Logan: You are not backing out of doing the challenge this weekend.

> Me: What makes you think I was even considering it??

I glance around to see if there are hidden cameras I'm not aware of. Maybe he's psychic? I hope not. If he knew the thoughts I had the other night, I'd never be able to look him in the eye again. Not that his eyes were the parts of his anatomy my fantasies focused on.

I write "batteries" on the grocery list hanging on my fridge. I should check into a BOB that charges with USB...

> Logan: Years of friendship.

> Me: What?

> Logan: Years of friendship tell me you're searching for reasons to skip doing the challenge this weekend and stay home. You probably told yourself the lighthouses aren't going anywhere and there's always next year.

> Me: Lol, well, I'm feeling called out. Fine, I'll go. But for the record, I had a rotten day at work. I have an injury.

My phone rings. Logan. Who else would it be?

"Logan?" I ask quizzically.

His deep voice is hard to hear over the crowd around him, but he sounds frantic.

"Are you okay? Did you go to the hospital? I'm so sorry for teasing you. Do you need anything?"

"I'm fine, Logan. It was just a paper cut. Just me being melodramatic. Sorry I worried you." I rest my forehead against the cool surface of the refrigerator.

I hear him let out a deep breath and say a quiet, "Thank God."

My heart does a funny little stutter step. "Hey, everything is okay. I'm being silly. Everything's fine. Why are you so upset?"

The crowd noise fades a bit. Where is he? Maybe a train station? I thought I heard a loudspeaker making announcements.

"I worry about something happening to you when I'm so far away," he says.

Forget a stutter step. My heart is doing a full-on cha-cha now because of the worry in his voice.

"Right back atcha, dude," I whisper softly.

My brain knows he's strong and competent. He isn't reckless, but some places he's gone and things he's done through the years have kept me up nights. Logan doesn't tell me about the sketchy situations he's encountered until after he comes home. That way I don't worry, but I'm petrified that someday I'm going to get the call that something has happened—he's been mugged in a dark alley or fallen off a mountain or been in an accident, and he's gone. Then I'd truly be all alone in the world. I don't know if I'd survive that.

"Daphne, I gotta go. Promise you'll do the lighthouse challenge this weekend. Even if you don't do the whole thing, do some of it each day. Go to Cape May on Sunday. You'll regret it if you don't."

"Where are you going? Are you at a train station? I'll do it and text you the selfies I take. Be careful." My turn to be the concerned friend.

Logan calls out to someone that he's coming. "I will. You be careful too. Talk to you soon. Watch out for deer and wet leaves. Bye."

I let out a shaky laugh. Gran used to say, "Bye, love ya, be careful. Watch out for deer and wet leaves," when we would leave her house after a visit. I hadn't thought about that in a while. Wet leaves and deer aren't all I need to watch out for. When he's concerned and protective of me like this, I can almost convince myself he feels more for me than friendship. I stop those thoughts though because the crash will hurt too much when it turns out we're still only friends.

8

LOGAN

Thank goodness for business class seating. The flight from London to Philadelphia would have been hell in coach. I'm too tall. It was easier to get a flight from Prague to London and then London to Philadelphia rather than try to fly directly from Prague to Philly. I thank the flight attendant for the tumbler of whiskey and get comfortable. Day drinking isn't my usual habit, but it's not like I'm driving in the next few hours.

I caught a late afternoon flight, so I'll arrive in the US before too late in the evening. I could go directly to Daphne's and surprise her so we could spend the weekend together, but it's best that she does this on her own. That she *knows* she can do this on her own.

I'm not a psychologist, but I think she's keeping herself in a small, little life because if she reaches out for more, she risks rejection, loss, disappointment, or maybe all three. She's so afraid of getting hurt more, she's choosing not to live to avoid the possibility of pain. She doesn't see that she's also closing herself off from the possibility of joy and love.

I love her so much it hurts. It hurts because I can't stand to see her timid and afraid to feel. However, I know I can't pull her into the light. I can only hold out my hand, so it's there when she's ready to take it and step out of the shadows. Luckily, photography's taught me the virtue of patience, waiting for light to be just right or elements to combine into a perfect tableau. Willingness to be patient makes the adequate extraordinary. The life I want with Daphne can be extraordinary. It's worth the wait.

I know my girl. She'll get there. I'm going to spend the flight thinking of my weekend plans and making notes on my phone.

"Excuse me, sir. Would you like another glass of whiskey?" I glance up at the purred question from the flight attendant. Her name tag says her name is Janet. Her green eyes remind me of a house cat with the way they tip at the corners. I suddenly feel like a field mouse on the menu for dinner.

"I would. Thank you, Janet." I accept the offered glass with a smile but do a double take at the napkin. She's written her phone number on it. When she comes to collect my empty glass, she sees the soiled napkin stuffed in the glass and raises a questioning glance at me. I allow a slight smile to touch my lips and turn my gaze back to my phone, where I've pulled up a picture of me and Daphne smiling, riding Wildwood's Ferris wheel with the sun glinting off the Atlantic in the background.

She gets the hint and moves on.

I'm relieved when my flight lands in Philadelphia. I'm one step closer to seeing Daphne, and we're finally on the same continent again. I grab an Uber to take me to my parents' home over the river in New Jersey. As we cross the Walt Whitman Bridge, I check my phone to see what new emails I have and if Daphne texted. She hasn't.

I texted Mom before I boarded my flight to let her know about my travel plans. After that one time we have all tacitly agreed to forget, I've learned the wisdom of letting my parents know when I'm coming by. With my younger brother Andy away at school, they like to take advantage of being empty nesters, and it's better for everyone to give notice of a visit. It's about half past seven when I let myself in the front door.

Dad calls from the kitchen, "Logan, right on time! We were getting ready to sit down for dinner, and now you can join us."

I inhale deeply. Sauce and garlic bread. Hot damn. It's pasta night. My mouth waters, and my stomach rumbles.

I drop my bags in the living room and wander back toward the kitchen and dining room. My mom is setting a third place at the table, knowing my inability to resist Dad's spaghetti sauce. For not having a drop of Italian blood in him, the man can do incredible things with tomatoes and garlic and whatever else he puts in there. If Dad ever gave up practicing law—he's an actual legal *eagle* because he's an eagle shifter like I am—he could make a killing with this sauce. I've asked him what his secret is, and he just winks. Winks! Those who know staid and serious Michael Morris in the office or the boardroom would be shocked to know marinara sauce moves him to winking.

They'd piss themselves laughing if they heard him giggle when Mom sidles up and says, "It's the love," in an almost sultry purr while pinching his ass.

I do not want to know the secret ingredient that badly. Seriously. I'll stick with the jarred stuff for my cooking.

"So, what brings you home, honey?" Mom asks, passing the basket filled with warm Italian bread.

"Would you believe a craving for Dad's sauce and your smile?"

Dad chuckles. "He got your nose, Holly, and my gift for bullshit. Nice try, Logan. Really, why are you home? Not that you aren't welcome. It's just a surprise."

I sigh, knowing it's best to just tell the truth. They'll get it out of me eventually. I don't know if it's the years of legal experience, parental intuition, shifter instinct, or that I suck at lying, but I've discovered it's less painful to tell them what they want to know—within reason—than to be evasive.

Here goes nothing. "I've come home to surprise Daphne and ask her to run away with me." I immediately stuff a large bite of bread in my mouth so I don't have to say anything more. I've already said too much.

My parents peer at each other. Pretty sure they're trying to decide whether I'm joking or if I'm serious. Fingers crossed, they go with joking. I don't think I'm going to be that lucky.

"Daphne Foster?" Dad queries. "Your friend from college that works for Morgan Development?"

Like we know a dozen Daphnes. "Yes, Dad, that Daphne."

We continue to eat in silence.

Now it's Mom's turn. "She's a nice girl."

More silence.

I can tell they're waiting for me to say more. It's killing them to wait me out. I take a sip of water. I rejected Mom's offer of wine since I already had two whiskeys on the flight. I need to keep a clear head for this conversation. I pick my fork up, twirling the linguine strands lazily.

Dad breaks first. "When you say, 'run away with you,' what do you mean?"

I eat my forkful of delicious pasta. "What it sounds like. I'm going to ask Daphne to travel with me. She's always wanted to travel. Her dream was to be a tour guide, see the world and share it with people."

"So why isn't she doing that?" Dad, asking the hard-hitting questions.

I sigh. "I told you, her parents died when she was in high school."

Mom nods, a sad expression crossing her face.

"They wanted her to be an accountant and carry on the family business," I continue. "You know how that goes. She majored in accounting and got straight A's, but she hated it. She did it because she knew that's what they would have wanted."

I take yet another sip of water and continue.

"She lived with her grandmother after they died, and they were very close. Gran urged her to take classes that would make her happy, like the history and architecture class we met in. When Gran died the summer before senior year, she left Daphne her house. Gran and I had discussed it was with the intention of it being sold, rented, or somehow used to fund her travels, but Daphne is using it as an anchor to keep her tied here."

Mom looks at me over the brim of her wine glass. "You left your work early, flew thousands of miles to tell a girl you like her, ask her to come away with you, and you don't know if she'll say yes?"

When she says it like that, I sound like an impulsive fool.

"I have it all planned. It will be fine."

"And what are her plans?" Dad asks quietly.

"I... I don't know. She hates her job." I grimace, remembering he's her boss. "Forget you heard that." At his nod, I continue. "She sits at home knitting and watching *Murder, She Wrote*. She doesn't leave the house unless she has to. If she wasn't working, I don't think she'd leave at all." I roll my shoulders. "I'm pretty sure she's a couple of weeks from ordering the Crazy Cat Lady Starter Kit from QVC."

My parents chuckle.

"I've asked her about going out with me before, but I think she thinks I'm kidding or being nice."

Mom waves her wineglass at me. "You always do this, Logan. You can't plan other people's lives out. Don't expect her to drop her entire life to do as you please."

"I don't!" I don't plan people's lives out. Not much anyway. Daphne will give a little, and I'll have to sacrifice too. It's how things work.

Besides, she's changing. This time, she'll be ready to go with me.

"I'm not," I insist. "There's not much joy traveling the world, seeing these spectacular sights and doing incredible things alone. I want her with me as my partner. My mate. I love her."

I take a deep breath. "I've loved her for years but didn't tell her because I don't want to ruin our friendship." I glance up at Mom. "In a different way, I'm afraid of risk like she is. But I'm willing to be the brave one if I win her in the end."

Mom blinks to hold glistening tears at bay.

Dad clears his throat. "Good. It's about time. So, what's your plan?"

9

DAPHNE

Saturday dawns with sunshine and fair weather. October in New Jersey is a bit of a crapshoot. There can be hurricanes or nor'easters, or the skies can be sunny and clear. The temperature can have you wearing a coat or shorts—sometimes on the same day because nature can be moody. Thankfully, this seems to be one of those perfect days—the sky is clear, the air has a slight chill, but the sun warms you. Most importantly, there are no mosquitoes.

No reason not to go. No more talking myself out of this. I know I need to do this. I need to dive into my past to move forward with my life. This was the last adventure I had with my parents before they died. Their accident was a few weeks later. Touring lighthouses one moment, holding back my tears at their funeral the next. I've been afraid to remember that weekend, the good times we had. Afraid to feel the sadness the memories will bring. I need to face the past if I'm going to move on to my future.

Driving north on the Garden State Parkway, I plan on being at the Sandy Hook Lighthouse right after it opens. According to the advertising, each location is giving away a crushed penny to commemorate the challenge. I still have the souvenir book from the first year we did the challenge. It's filled with wooden nickels. They burned the likeness of each lighthouse on a coin.

I pull into the parking lot, take a sip of water, and apply my lipstick. I chuckle at primping for a selfie, but whatever. This shade is "Wine with Everything." My preference is rum with Diet Pepsi, but any port in a storm. I lock my Escape and approach the table to pick up my souvenirs.

"Good morning! Welcome to Sandy Hook, the last remaining colonial lighthouse," the volunteer says in greeting. "Will you be climbing the tower today?"

I collect my coin and buy my keepsake book. "Good morning. No climb for me. I enjoy staying on terra firma. Not a fan of tight spaces or heights." I peruse the challenge commemorative T-shirts for sale and decide to buy a set for me and Logan. Logan's is to make up for all the shirts I've stolen from him.

After leaving a donation, I wander off to find a suitable spot to take my picture. I feel silly sending inexpertly shot selfies to a professional photographer, but he asked for it. I smile and take the shot. It's awkward as hell. I caption it, "Greetings from Sandy Hook, the last remaining colonial lighthouse," hit send, and off it goes.

I drive south to my next stops, the Twin Lights in Highlands and Sea Girt, stopping at Wawa for snacks. The girl behind the counter, Donna, according to her name tag, smacks her gum. "You're excited."

I grin. I can't help it. "I'm doing the lighthouse challenge today." I practically bounce on my toes.

Donna lifts her brows, smirking. "Lighthouses?" Her tone is an eye roll. "Exciting."

"It is! Lighthouses are romantic! My grandparents first confessed their love for one another in one. And my father proposed to my mother in one too." Using the worthless Cape May diamond quartz stones that wash up on the beach there. I sigh. He was poor. It was romantic.

But the girl seems bored.

"Lighthouses are lovely," I grumble, pocketing my card.

"Yeah, whatever." I doubt Donna wins many customer service awards.

When I return to my car, I open the box of Entenmann's glazed Pop'ems I bought. When my parents and I did this trip, food pickings were slim in a few stretches, so provisions were necessary. They're necessary now too, so I'm well-prepared with peanut butter and jelly sandwiches and bottled water I brought from home, plus the donut holes and bag of Munchos I just bought. An adventure is no time to give up on carbs.

I continue south to visit the Sea Girt lighthouse. It's truly a house with a light on it. When I was a girl, I remember being fascinated by the thought of living in a lighthouse and the adventure it would be. This would be the style I'd want. No curving spiral staircases to fall through, no nauseating heights. It's a simple, lovely red-brick home that has helped save lives. Sounds perfect.

When I last did the challenge as a sixteen-year-old, I didn't appreciate the beauty of the lighthouse. All I saw was the Sea Girt boardwalk and beach across the street, imagining it was probably full of shirtless guys all summer long.

What a difference in perspective ten years brings. After getting my coin and picking up a ceramic magnet depicting the lighthouse, I cross Ocean Avenue and climb the boardwalk's steps.

This boardwalk isn't like boardwalks in the towns further south, in Atlantic City and Wildwood. No amusement piers or casinos, no saltwater taffy shops...at least not at this end. I've never walked the length of it, so I don't know for sure, but it doesn't seem like there are businesses along it. I should bring my bike up here and ride the boards. Depending on when Logan comes back, maybe we can do it together. It's a change of pace from what we're used to. The southern Jersey shore towns we hang out in are usually full of tourists. There, the combined scents of pizza, sunscreen, and ocean air tickle the nose. The neon lights on the casinos and piers draw the eye and distract you from the beach and the vast Atlantic Ocean just across the sand. Here, it's quieter, calmer, and the Atlantic with its never-ending ebb and flow is the star of the show. I can feel the salt in the breeze that blows off the water, but I'm not being jostled by the crowd or enticed to enter arcades and shops. Because there aren't any. It's the beach and the ocean. And peace. I love it.

I take my picture with the unassuming brick structure in the background. With its tidy lawn and welcoming porch, it's such a pleasant house. It would be so cool to raise a family in a lighthouse, even a decommissioned one. The lens room at the top would make a glorious spot to sit and read, or maybe relax with wine at the end of a long day. We could tell our children stories about shipwrecks and rescues. Logan would show them pictures from his travels.

Wait.

When did I start imagining Logan as my hypothetical children's father? We're friends. He's my *best* friend. We aren't getting married or having children together. He's never here.

A little voice in my head reminds me I could always go with him. I tell her to sit back down and shut up. He doesn't think of me as anything more than a friend, so there's no point thinking about a future together.

Thinking about the future is pointless, anyway. My parents had plans for the future, and look how that turned out. My fingers tremble a bit when I type in the message to go with the picture: "Sea Girt. Wish you were here." Before I can change my mind, I hit send and get in my car to continue southward.

After visiting the Barnegat and Tucker's Island Lighthouses, I end my day at the Absecon Lighthouse in Atlantic City. It blows my mind that this majestic lighthouse is in the middle of an urban neighborhood, just blocks away from the glittering lights of the casinos. Do the locals take it for granted? Probably. It's always been there and will always be there as far as they're concerned. Like everyone has an almost two-hundred-foot lighthouse in their backyard.

After I pick up my coin, I decide to buy a postcard showing an aerial view of the lighthouse at twilight with the ocean and casinos in the background. The juxtaposition of the stately white-and-black tower against the neon glow of Atlantic City is jarring. It's like Queen Elizabeth hanging with a group of Vegas showgirls. I snort-laugh and draw curious glances from the volunteers.

I smile and say, "Long day."

They laugh in return and agree, telling me it's been a great day and something they look forward to every year.

"Please take a picture of me?" I ask the volunteers on a whim. I figure I should try to send at least one decent picture of myself to Logan today.

"I'll do it." A friendly man in his fifties steps from behind the table and holds out his hand for my camera. His name tag says Jeff. With salt-and-pepper hair and glasses, he resembles a dad. My dad was getting a bit of early gray at his temples when he died. I wonder if he'd be salt-and-pepper like Jeff or all gray?

"Ready?" Jeff asks. When I smile and say yes, he takes my picture.

I take back my phone. "Thank you." I drop a few bills in the donation jar and head home.

It's been a long day, but it's been a good one. I'm surprised. I thought I'd be much more emotional and despondent, revisiting places I'd gone to with my parents. They have been on my mind a lot today, but while I've been sad to not have them here with me, my memories have been happy ones. It's a relief. That's what they would want for me, to remember them and feel happy, not to feel the over-whelming grief and loss that's been my near-constant companion all these years.

I send the last picture from today when I get home.

Logan responded with a thumbs up after Barnegat, so he's seen them. He must be busy traveling or working on whatever his current assignment is. I'm sure I'll hear from him later. Being brilliant and lazy, I picked up fast food on the way home. I finish my fries while checking out Logan's Instagram feed, flicking through all the places he's traveled.

My favorite out of all his locations has been Ireland. It was so green but also rugged. I would love to go there someday. Maybe I could sit in a pub and listen to the cadence of the voices. Maybe they'd burst into song, like what happens in my favorite books by Nora Roberts. That would be magical. He hasn't done many shoots in the United States or Canada. Everything has been oceans away. Maybe if he had assignments on this continent, I could join him. I don't think he made his offers to accompany him out of pity or because he knew I'd turn him down.

I'm sure he wants me to join him. As his friend. Good old buddy Daphne.

It's barely nine, but I prepare for bed and shake thoughts of the future away. They bring nothing but pain, disappointment, more loneliness. The past is comfortable, safe. And tomorrow, I can return to it. More lighthouses, more memories of my parents. More adventure.

10

LOGAN

I STUDY THE PICTURES DAPHNE SENT ME OF HER ADVENTURES TODAY. SHE seems happier than I've seen her in years. My heart constricted when I read her "Wish you were here" message. I'm working on it, honey. Besides the selfies, she included a picture she took of a bench at the base of the Barnegat Lighthouse. On the bench is a plaque bearing names with a date and the words "He asked - she said yes." It had to remind her of hearing about her dad's proposal to her mom at the Cape May Lighthouse. We're going to have a bench of our own some-day. I know it.

I imagine all the places around the world we could have benches and plaques to commemorate the special moments of our lives. Our first kiss, our first time telling each other "I love you," where I propose, where we go on our tenth anniversary. I can't wait to show our kids the special spots and tell them the stories. Just as Daphne's parents and grandparents told her about their stories with the Cape May Lighthouse, we'll be able to tell our kids the story of how we shared special times not only at the Cape May Lighthouse but all around the world too.

We could travel in the summer when the kids are off from school.

I'm curious if Daphne would want to homeschool. That way, we could travel with the kids without the restriction of school calendars. That's years down the road though. We need a few years of just us before we have kids. At least two kids. It would be so cool to teach them to fly if they were eagle shifters like me. I could show them so many things.

I finish the editing project I'm working on and get ready for bed. Tomorrow is a big day, and I want to be well-rested for it. If I'm lucky, I won't get much sleep tomorrow night.

11

DAPHNE

Sunday is another picture-perfect day. I start the day at the lighthouses on the Delaware River and am working my way along the coast of the Delaware Bay, my favorite part of the trip. The drive along the western and southern coasts of New Jersey is so peaceful. When people think of New Jersey, they think of casinos or turnpikes or super tan dudes with big muscles strutting along the boardwalk. They don't think of these tranquil places where you can be quiet. I love driving the backroads, especially in the fall when the leaves are changing.

I arrive at East Point Lighthouse around noon. The East Point Lighthouse from my memory is crumbling. Paint flaking off everywhere, swirling in the ever-present wind coming in through the sizable gaps created by the missing tiles in the fabled red roof. *This* East Point Lighthouse is beautiful, nothing like my memory but still familiar. The white exterior is brighter, the red roof complete and vibrant in the midday sun. No longer are guests limited to one room. The entire house-like structure is available to explore, all the way up to the light tower extending out the roof. It sits on the Delaware Bay's edge, surrounded by marshland. I've read in the news about coastal storms eroding the dunes erected to protect the lighthouse. The preservation group has been working hard to get governmental help.

"Wow," I say, collecting my souvenir. "You've done a wonderful job with the restoration. The last time I was here was ten years ago, and it needed so much work."

The gentlemen at the table puff up with pride.

"Thank you, young lady. It's been a labor of love. Now if we can get the help we need to curb the erosion, we'll have a chance at protecting this beauty."

"I hope you're successful. It would be a tragedy to lose this wonderful lighthouse."

As I tour the renovated interior and examine the antiques collected to decorate the home, Lantern, the lighthouse kitty, rubs against my leg.

"Hey, kitty," I croon as I pet its head. I smile at the purr that emanates from her. Him? We'll stick with kitty. Maybe I should get a cat. It would be nice to have company. After collecting my coin and donating, I grab my lunch from the car and sit on a bench near the dunes. It's so peaceful here. Even with groups of people coming and going today, there's a sense of serenity and timelessness.

What would it have been like to be a lighthouse keeper or the keeper's wife out here in this bit of heaven? Would it have been lonely? Or wonderful? I can't imagine being here while a storm raged. Thunder and lightning must be louder and brighter without other buildings around. There would be waves crashing on shore, threatening to breach the dunes and rush to the steps of your home. With all the marshland, there must be times you're cut off from the nearest town. Sure, it's a small town, but it would offer at least a touch of civilization. I'm probably best suited for my quiet, suburban life. I don't know if the romance of living in a lighthouse is enough to overcome my scaredy-cat tendencies.

I brought my binoculars with me for bald eagle or dolphin spotting. I've read both are visible here, but no luck so far. Maybe it's the wrong time of year? I want to come back when there aren't as many people around. Possibly I'll have success then. I'll ask Logan. He'd know.

Has he ever flown here? I've known for years he's an eagle shifter, but we've never discussed details. He's the first shifter I met, well, that I know is a shifter. When we were growing up, shifters and other paranormal folk were still a secret. When I was in high school, a bride on one of the cable television wedding shows got so mad over something minor, she shifted into a grizzly bear on camera. They named that episode "Grizzilla." Since then, it's come out that shifters, vampires, witches, and other paranormal creatures have always lived among us peacefully. They've been our teachers, doctors, clergy, best friends. It's amazing it was a secret for so long.

Reality TV was quick to jump in the fray with shows like *Bigfoot Finds a Bride*, a dating show my friend Shelby was on, and *Yeti Get Ready*, a makeover show. My favorite is *From Dud to Den*, a home makeover program on cable. I love how they tie natural elements into the designs. I love watching these shows, but it's intimidating how beautiful the shifter girls are even when they're a hot mess in need of a makeover. I wish I had the confidence they exude. On the shifter dating shows, the successful relationships often only happen when both of the contestants are shifters. The season Shelby was on *Bigfoot Finds a Bride*, the Bigfoot bachelor ended up cutting Shelby, who truly cared about him, only to end up being rejected by the human woman he picked to propose to because she had the wrong idea about shifters. Thankfully, he and Shelby found each other again recently and are in love. Liam's parents are a mixed marriage. His mom is human and his dad shifts. They're happy, but they might be the exception that proves the rule. It helps that his mom, Faith, is gorgeous and smart. Heck, she was a cheerleader for the Philadelphia football team. She may be human, but she's more than just a regular woman.

I see the sign directing me to the next lighthouse and hit my blinker.

After spending a restful hour at East Point, I begin my trip to my ultimate destination: Cape May Point and the Cape May Lighthouse. I drum my fingers on the steering wheel as I drive along, inexpertly keeping time with the beat of Van Halen's "Jump." When it was Dad's turn to pick the music on a road trip, it would always be their 1984 album.

I alternate between being excited to visit again and dreading facing these memories. I've avoided so many experiences these past ten years since my parents passed because I don't want to feel the sorrow of doing it alone. I've fought hard to climb out of the well of despair I was wallowing in.

I resisted going to therapy and was angry when Gran insisted I go. When I finally gave in, I just sat there for fifty minutes in stony silence. I'm ashamed to admit that the first few weeks, that's all I did. Eventually, I connected with my therapist, Claire, and she helped me so much. I still check in every few months for a tune-up.

I struggle with catastrophizing. I expect everything to go wrong and to be awful. It's a defense mechanism. If I expect the worst, I'm not blindsided again when it happens. I wasn't like this when I was younger. I was such an optimist, when one of my teachers told me I was obnoxiously perky, I took it as a compliment.

Then the accident happened, and I buried that optimist with my parents.

But I'm going to bring her back. Claire is going to be proud of me for doing this, and I'm looking forward to telling her.

I wish I wasn't doing this alone. I know I can do it on my own, but I don't want to. I hope to find love one day and have someone to share adventures with. Logan, preferably. However, it won't be today. And it won't be at the lighthouse. And it definitely won't be him.

"Oh, thank goodness," I mutter, pulling into the Cape May Lighthouse parking lot and seeing the sign pointing to the bathrooms. Real bathrooms, not porta-potties like at the last two stops. The lighthouse is part of a state park with hiking trails, picnic pavilions, and a visitor center. There's a viewing platform overlooking a pond. Being at New Jersey's southern tip, the area is an important stop for migratory birds and a bird-watcher's paradise.

As I step out of the restroom onto the deck, I see an enormous bird, some kind of raptor, resting on a branch. I'm uncertain what kind it is, but it makes think me of Logan. I've never seen him as his golden eagle shifter. I've never knowingly seen anyone in their shifter form in person, just on TV.

I bet my parents would know exactly what kind of bird it is and tell me all about its habitat, migratory habits, and other things. Mom's big thing was to talk about breeding plumage. Mom was a bit of a goof. I got that from her. I smile, realizing I've been smiling at memories of my parents this weekend, not tearing up. This adventure has been what I've needed to help me move on. I'm always going to miss them, but they're still with me, no matter where I am. They would want me to be happy and live my life to the fullest. I think I'm finally ready to do that. I don't know how yet, but I'll figure it out.

The pair of ladies at the volunteer table are staring at me. I hope I wasn't talking to myself again. I rub my nose in case of boogers. They're whispering to each other, and the shorter one excitedly waves to me. I give a tentative wave back and walk their way. There's been a nice, steady crowd while I've been here, so it's not like they're lacking company. I guess they're super friendly, and that's a wonderful trait to have when dealing with the public, I guess. Maybe that's not water in their bottles? I bet this could be a lot more fun with a buzz on.

"Hello," I say, approaching the table.

The taller one—her name tag says Maggie—greets me with a big smile. "Hello! How are you today?"

"I'm well, thank you. How are you?"

The shorter one, Joan, responds. "We're great, thank you, dear. I always love the lighthouse challenge weekend and seeing familiar faces from years past. We've seen kids grow up through the years, and they're bringing their own families to visit. It's exciting."

A wistful smile crosses my face. I hope to bring my children here someday, where my parents brought me. A little boy with green eyes and dark brown hair like his daddy, maybe a little girl too.

"Thanks," I say when Joan hands me my coin. I turn and take out my phone so I can get my picture.

Maggie says, "Oh! You must take a picture with the lighthouse keeper!" She points to a banner that says, "I visited the Cape May Lighthouse!" set up in front of the lighthouse with a gentleman dressed in an old-fashioned lighthouse keeper's uniform standing nearby. A couple has just had their picture taken and are walking away after thanking him. It appears there's a volunteer on hand to take pictures using the visitors' phones. It's a cool idea. There's a donation bucket set up alongside him. Brilliant fundraising on their part. I give my phone to Jim, the picture taker, and walk over to the keeper and stand on his left side. He's an older gentleman, probably in his mid-sixties, with white hair and a beard. He has twinkling blue eyes and a bit of a belly. Wow, I've discovered what Santa does in the off-season.

"Hello," the keeper says kindly.

"Hi," I reply. "This is a great idea."

Maggie and Joan wander over and stand next to Jim, practically vibrating with excitement. There must be something extra in their water bottles. Jim takes our picture, and when I go to move away, he calls out to stay there. He wants to take one more. The keeper apparently didn't hear him because he walks away. Maybe Jim means to take a shot of just me? Whatever.

I see the enormous bird from before flying by. Wow, it's huge. I'd bet it has a wingspan of at least six feet. It's beautiful how the late afternoon sunlight glistens off the burnished golden feathers on its head. The brown feathers on its body almost look like velvet. Being a raptor, I'm sure it has sharp talons, and that hooked beak disabuses any notion of cuddliness, but I'm drawn to it anyway. I turn to watch it fly, but Jim calls for me to face him.

I smile and obey, ready for him to snap the picture, when I feel someone walk up behind me and place their arm around my shoulders. I turn, ready to knock out the creep that has snuck up on me. My brain registers the delicious scent of bay rum before my eyes tell me I'm looking at the smiling, painfully dear handsome face that holds my heart.

"What are you doing here?" I cry, reaching up to hug Logan. "Wait, was that you that just flew by?"

His powerful arms close around me, and his lips brush my cheek. I love being hugged by Logan. He's so tall and broad. He makes me feel small and delicate. When I'm in his arms, I'm cherished and safe. I rest my head against his shoulder and relish being held by him. I don't know if it was thirty seconds or five minutes, but we finally break apart. Jim hands me back my phone and pulls Joan and Maggie away to give us a bit of privacy. They keep glancing over their shoulders at us as they walk back to their table.

Logan takes my hand and leads me away from the photo area. We sit on a bench in the lighthouse's shadow, under a bunch of pine trees. He turns toward me and takes my hand, his beautiful green gaze meeting mine. "Yeah, that was me. I know how important the Cape May Lighthouse is to your family's story, and I wanted to join you here so you—we could add a chapter to it. Open your email."

I open the email app on my phone and see a message from him has just come in, and it has an attachment. When I open it, I see a collage of the selfies I took at each of the earlier lighthouses I visited. But he's photoshopped himself into each shot, so it appears he's standing next to me.

With a shaky breath passing through my lips, I gaze up at him. "What is this?"

"I hope it's a peek at our future." Logan rests his palm on my cheek. "Daphne, sweetheart, you're precious to me. You have been since the moment we met. I didn't know what to do about it then, but now I do. I want to be with you. I don't want to keep traveling and leaving you behind. There are lighthouses all over the country, all over the world. Maybe we can take trips to some of them together. I just want us to be together. Be mine?"

I cover his hand with my own. "Oh, Logan. I can't believe you're here. I...I wasn't expecting this." I take a shuddering breath. "Wow."

I don't know what to say. What does he mean when he says he wants to be with me? Is he staying here with me? Is he expecting me to go with him? My brain isn't supplying any words, but my heart says what to do. I lean forward and place my lips on his. In the background, Maggie and Joan cheer.

12

LOGAN

I don't know how long Daphne and I sit on that bench, kissing and talking, but the park the lighthouse is in closes at dusk, so it's time we leave.

"Are you riding with me?" Daphne asks as we approach her car. "I assume you flew down here?"

"Nope, I drove down. I'm parked over there." I point to a spot near the entrance to walking trails where I parked my Jeep. "I can't carry my wallet and phone if I fly, and I needed to follow along on your adventures today. I shifted when I got here and waited on that branch so I could see when you arrived and surprise you. I created quite a stir." I preen. "You know Cape May is a mecca for birders, so to have a fine golden eagle specimen like myself hanging out for the afternoon put a star on quite a few birders' life lists."

I regret my decision to drive my car since that means we'll drive home separately. I hate being apart from her for even a moment now that I have her. I should have Ubered. I give her one more kiss and force myself to pull back. I can't not touch her, so allow my hand to linger on her cheek.

"We need to go home." I consider her house my home since

that's where I stay when I'm in the country. It didn't make sense to rent an apartment that I wouldn't be in often. I could stay at my parents' house, but I'd always rather be with Daphne. We hang out and watch movies. She puts up with me watching baseball and cheering way too loudly for the Phillies, and I pretend to be interested in the DVR full of Hallmark Christmas movies. We both enjoy watching rugby and hockey together. I watch the play, but I'm pretty sure she's checking out the rugby thighs and hockey butts. We both cheer for the Flyers and have attended games together over the years. Maybe we can get to a couple this year. I'll have to check the schedule to see if they're home before I leave on my next trip in just over a week.

"And we need dinner," I say. "Do you want to stop somewhere?"

She stares at me a bit dreamily with her deep brown gaze. Our kisses affected her as much as they did me. "I like it that you call my house home. I need dinner, but I don't want to stop anywhere to sit and eat. We can get takeout or delivery."

"Honey, once we're behind closed doors, I don't want to see anyone but you for the rest of the night, at least. No delivery people, no friends, nobody, just me and you. If we're getting food, we're getting it before we get home. What do you want? Pizza? Burgers? Chinese?" I can't help my smirk when I consider what I want to do once I have her alone.

Daphne must be able to read the thoughts on my face because she declares, "Pizza. It'll be good for breakfast too." Ah, a woman after my own heart.

We walk hand in hand to her car. We decide I'll pick up pizza from our favorite shop and meet at home. I get in my car and follow her out of the parking lot, and we head toward the heart of Cape May so we can go through town and get on the Parkway to drive north toward home. I use voice control to call Daphne.

"Hello?"

"I'd like to speak to my girlfriend, please."

She giggles. "I'm your girlfriend?"

"Considering you spent an hour making out with me on that bench and now you're luring me back to your lair to, hopefully, take advantage of my virtue, you damn well better be my girlfriend. What kind of man do you take me for?"

More giggles. "You're such a goober."

"I'm *your* goober."

She sighs. "I still can't believe you're here. I'm afraid my alarm is going to go off and I'll wake up and realize this was all just a dream. If that's what this is, it's going to break my heart because it feels so real."

My heart clenches at hearing her vulnerability.

"Daphne, if this is a dream, it's a dream we're both having. It's real. When your alarm goes off, I'll be there." There's silence on the line. I peek at my dash to make sure the call's still connected. "Daph?"

"I'm here. Do you have E-ZPass for the toll?"

We're approaching a toll booth. The miles are passing quickly, thank goodness.

"I do. Go through the express lane." I don't know what brought about that change of subject. Another mile or two passes.

"Logan, we're getting close to home. Did you want to call and order the pizza now so it's ready to pick up?"

Okay, we *are* changing the subject. "Sure. Did you want anything other than pizza?"

"Soda, if you want something other than Diet Pepsi. I don't have any wine or beer." I hear her take a deep breath. "Okay, I'll let you go so you can order. See you at home. Drive safely."

"Daphne?"

"Yeah?"

"See you soon." Those weren't the three words I wanted to say, but I don't know if she's ready to hear "I love you" from me.

I disconnect and then call in our order at the pizza place. I order a plain cheese pizza for Daphne and a pepperoni and sausage for myself. Not that either of us is eating a whole pizza tonight, but I don't want to leave the house for a couple of days. We need to keep our strength up. I thought about garlic knots, but considering how much kissing I plan on doing, maybe that isn't the best choice. I add a chicken Caesar salad for lunch tomorrow. After placing our order, I contemplate what's bugging Daphne. She seemed to get quiet suddenly. We reach our exit and take the off-ramp. She turns right to head to the house, and I make a left to get dinner.

13
DAPHNE

I RUSH AROUND THE HOUSE WITH NO IDEA WHAT TO DO WITH MYSELF. IT'S times like this I wish I had one of those long, low, fancy couches made for swooning. I need to swoon. Or faint. Okay, I've settled on hyperventilating.

Oh my goodness. Logan is back in New Jersey, and he wants me to be his. What does that even mean? He'll be here in ten minutes, and staying here, and we're a couple, and I don't know what the hell I'm doing. I've never done this.

Do we eat dinner and then go to bed?

Crap, I didn't shave my legs this morning.

Five minutes. Do I have time to shave everything? Do I change into lingerie? Wait, I don't have lingerie.

Shoot, I'm so not ready for this.

"Hi, honey, I'm home!" Logan walks in with the pizza boxes and a bag hanging off his wrist.

"I got a pizza for each of us, so we have leftovers, Caesar salad for lunch tomorrow, and root beer. I've been craving root beer. Where do you want to eat? Table or couch?"

I stand there staring at him.

"Daph? You okay?"

I give a weak smile and head into the kitchen to get us plates and glasses. "I'm fine. Let's sit at the table."

As I reach into the cabinet to get our plates, I feel his hands at my waist. He brushes a kiss on my neck, and although I can't control my shiver, I tense up. Taking the plates from my hands and setting them on the counter, Logan then puts a hand on my hip to turn me around to face him.

I lean against the counter and gaze up at him. I've never noticed how much taller than me he is. I mean, I've always known Logan has several inches on me, but this is the first time we've been this close face-to-face without something else happening, like laughing or hugging.

"Honey, talk to me. I know something is going on in your beautiful mind. What is it?" A concerned expression passes over his face, and he backs up, glancing away. "Have you changed your mind? I surprised you. If you're having second thoughts about this, just tell me."

I don't know what to say, so I stand there like an idiot. I can't even look up at him any longer. I'm staring at his white T-shirt with the red heart on it.

Logan exhales, and I swear it came from the depths of his soul. "Okay, um, I'm going to grab a couple of slices and go to my room." He reaches past me, the combination of his arm brushing my shoulder and a whiff of his sexy scent almost knocking me over. Logan is leaving.

"Wait...what?" I sound like an idiot, but I have no clue what is going on.

"Daphne, something's going on. You're not talking to me, and I can tell I'm making you uncomfortable. That's the last thing I want to do. I know I sprung all this on you, and we got a bit carried away. I guess you're regretting it now. I can stay at my parents' tonight if you'd prefer. I was going to leave in the morning, but I can go now."

My heart sinks, and tears flood my eyes. My first boyfriend, and he's ready to break up after two hours. I knew I couldn't do this.

"Hey, don't cry. Talk to me."

His thumb brushes away the tear sliding down my cheek. I whisper, "I don't know what to do." Death by embarrassment must not really be a thing because I'm still breathing. I rest my head against his chest and wrap my arms around his waist. Hearing Logan's heart thumping under my ear is comforting, and the warmth of his arms around me is heavenly. It's easier to talk if I'm not looking at him.

"Do about what?"

I feel the rumble of the words against my cheek as well as hear them. With a sigh, I respond, "How to do this. I've never done this before. I'm afraid I'm not going to be good at it."

We stand there, Logan's thumb brushing along my spine. It feels so good that I want to purr like a cat. That would probably be weird.

He pulls away and takes my hand. "C'mon, let's sit on the couch. We need to talk."

I've watched enough TV to know nothing good comes from that phrase. We sit side by side. Logan still holds my hand, and he turns toward me. I'm staring straight ahead, afraid of what I'm going to see if I face him. I was so close to having what I wanted, and I'm losing it already.

"Daphne, look at me. Honey, what's going on?"

I turn to peek at him. He's so handsome. I don't want to screw this up.

"I don't know what I'm doing. I've never done this before."

He rests his hand against my cheek, and it's so warm. "When you say you haven't done this before, what exactly do you mean? Just tell me."

I guess I have to put it all out there. The bouncing of my leg is making the whole couch shake. Does Logan notice? "I don't know how to have a relationship. I don't know how to be a girlfriend. I don't know how to have a boyfriend. I know nothing. I've done none of this before." I lift my face to him.

Logan gazes back with a crease between his brows and a confused puppy head tilt. His thumb still caresses my cheek though, so that's nice. His hand leaves my face and rests against the back of the couch. Well, it was nice while it lasted.

I go to stand. May as well eat some pizza. But before I can get up all the way, Logan has hooked my belt loop and pulled me back down alongside him.

His arm wraps around my shoulders, and he leans toward me. "Hey, it's okay."

I lift my gaze.

He's smiling gently at me. "Daphne, are you a virgin?"

My skin goes hot, and I lower my face.

"No, no, no, look at me. It's okay. It's me. You can tell me anything. Daphne, come on."

Okay, deep breath, be brave. I meet his gaze. "Yes, I'm a virgin, and this is a lot, and I wasn't expecting it. You know I have a hard time with surprises, even wonderful ones, and I don't know what to do, and I don't want to be bad at it, and you know what you're doing, and I didn't shave my legs today. Oh my God! You're laughing at me!"

That's it, I'm out of here. Logan's grip tightens around my shoulders before I can stand.

"No! Honey, I'm not laughing at you. I mean, not in any kind of bad way. We're good. We go at your speed. As long as you're not channeling your inner Chewbacca, I don't care what your legs are like. I didn't shave mine today either."

My shoulders relax. I didn't realize how tight they'd been.

"A lot has happened today," he says, "and I've had the advantage of knowing that I'd see you. Let's take a deep breath, eat our pizza, and relax. Nothing needs to happen tonight. We're just us, same as always."

Giggling, I can't resist. "Us but with kissing." I hope just kissing is enough for him. I'm not ready to jump headfirst into all the other physical aspects of our relationship yet.

14

LOGAN

THIS WASN'T HOW I WAS EXPECTING THE NIGHT TO GO. I IMAGINED US cuddling on the couch, but in my fantasy, there was more making out and less yelling at the refs for penalty calls against the Flyers. Daphne is so sweet, but put a hockey game on the TV, and she goes into beast mode. Philly is playing Boston, so it's a hard-hitting, fast-skating game, with both teams generating penalties, something Daphne is taking personally.

"C'mon! That was a trip! Where's the call? What do we need for you to call in our favor? Gritty blow you during intermission?"

I shudder at the thought of that but laugh. She's hilarious to watch a game with. When we go to games in Philly, I make sure she only drinks soda, and I keep her full of snacks because mixing hockey and a hangry, drunk Daphne is not a good thing.

We're sitting on the couch, and Daph is snuggling up against me with my arm around her shoulder. The bowl of Chicago mix popcorn rests on her lap. This feels comfortable. I wasn't expecting us to have sex tonight. I wouldn't mind at all if we did, of course, but I figured we'd take things slowly. Not this slowly though. There are glaciers moving faster than this. *This* reminds me of being a teenager.

Huh. If Daphne is as inexperienced as I assume she is after her earlier outburst, she might be at *the-teenager-watching-TV-on-the-couch* stage of things. Okay, how did I do this at fifteen?

I brush my fingertips along her arm where my hand rests around her shoulder. She shivers, and goosebumps rise on her skin. She's responsive. That's good. I angle my head to nuzzle her temple and place a tender kiss there. She sighs, and her lashes flutter. I snag a handful of popcorn and turn my attention back to the game.

Daphne peeks at me for a moment before also focusing on the game again.

There are only four minutes left in the first period. I can be patient.

She leans forward and places the bowl on the coffee table, then snuggles deeper into my side. I tighten my arm around her shoulder and watch the seconds tick down, marking the end of the period.

She gets up from the couch, grabs her glass, and looks at me. "Do you want anything to drink? I'm going to get a bit more soda."

"No, I'm good," I say, standing as well. "Be right back." I lean to place a quick kiss on her lips and place my hand on her hip when I shift past her in the space between the coffee table and couch. After I brush my teeth and change into an old T-shirt and gray sweatpants I have in my dresser in the second bedroom, I grab a blanket and pillow off the bed I use when I stay here and return to the living room. I see Daphne had a similar idea and changed into a tee and blue sleep shorts with cartoon sheep on them. Her shirt is from a co-ed softball league we were in during college. She has her own team T-shirt, but seeing my last name on her back stirs something possessive in me. I enjoy seeing my name on her very much. It belongs there.

"Great minds think alike," I murmur.

"And fools seldom differ," Daphne finishes the familiar phrase with a grin.

I spread the blanket over the back of the sofa and lie down.

She quirks her head. "Where am I supposed to sit?"

I pat my chest. "Lie right here. We're cuddling while watching the rest of the game."

Her skeptical expression cracks me up. I shift to my side and press my back against the rear cushions.

"Fine, we'll do it this way. Don't worry. I'll make sure you don't fall off. I'll hold on to you."

"I bet," she mutters. But she settles against me.

I reach back and pull the blanket over us, then wrap my arm around her waist and pull her snugly against me. Her hair is in a low ponytail and pours over the bicep of the arm I have folded under our heads. It's silky, smelling of strawberries and vanilla. I'm suddenly craving strawberry shortcake. Daphne wiggles a bit, getting comfortable as the Flyers face off against the Bruins to start the second period. Her curvy ass nestles against my crotch, and my cock stirs in interest. Maybe this wasn't the best idea.

Daphne sighs and relaxes against me. "I never thought we'd be here like this, Logan. This has been the best day of my life. Thank you."

I brush a kiss on her shoulder. "Best day so far. There will be more even better than this. Trust me."

She burrows more deeply under the blanket and against me. "I can't wait."

Okay, this was a good idea.

This is the calmest Daph has ever been watching a hockey game. If she hadn't yelled at the refs for a bad call against the Flyers' center, I'd think she'd fallen asleep. Gritty is dancing in the stands as the Flyers leave the ice going into the second intermission. He's a happy...I'm not sure what he is. A deranged Muppet? But it doesn't matter because Philly is beating Boston four to one.

Daphne stirs and turns to face me, draping one arm over my waist and reaching up to caress my cheek with her other hand. I unfold my bottom arm to embrace her fully and pull her closer to me. We both give in to the temptation and indulge in a kiss.

I don't know how we went all those years without doing this. It's addicting. Her lips are so soft and pliant, and I trace her lower lip with my tongue, seeking admission into her sweet mouth. Our tongues dance, and her hand moves up my back to caress my nape and play with the hair brushing the collar of my T-shirt, while mine moves lower to palm her ass and press her tighter against me. My cock stiffens, and I long to press it against her sweet warmth, but that's too much, too fast for my girl. It would be oh so easy to keep kissing and let hormones, lust, and love, at least on my part, sweep us away. But Daphne isn't ready for that yet, and if we got carried away tonight, it wouldn't be fair to our relationship. I'm in this for the long haul. I can be patient. We haven't said it yet, but I know I love Daphne, and she's worth waiting for.

No one has ever actually died from sexual frustration, right?

I soften our kiss and pull back slightly, gazing into unfocused, lust-glazed pools of molten chocolate. Somehow Daphne has ended up on her back, and I'm half covering her with my body. It would be so easy to lower my head and pick up where we left off, but I push up off the couch. I'm tenting my sweat pants, but there's nothing to do about it now. I back up so my cock isn't right at eye level when she sits up. I'd love to introduce them to each other, but now is not the time.

The roar of the crowd on TV pulls my attention and gives me the excuse to turn and face the screen while I try to get my erection under control. The last period of the hockey game has started.

"Do you want to keep watching?" I ask her.

Her nimble fingers braid the hair she has pulled over her shoulder. She's doing this to have something to focus on while deciding how to answer. I know her so well. At least, I think I do. She hunts for and finds the elastic tie I had slipped from her tresses while we kissed and uses it to secure her work.

"No," she finally says, "I'm good. I'll catch the highlights tomorrow if anything exciting happens. I have to get up for work anyway."

I didn't think about her having to work tomorrow.

"Do you have to go in? Can you call out?"

"No, I can't call out," she says a bit testily. "Mallory took off on Friday. I had to cover things she normally handles, so I didn't get to do everything I needed to for my own duties. I need tomorrow to get back on track."

I run my hand through my hair. "I'm here until next Monday, and then I have to head to Portugal and Spain. How's your Spanish? There are so many places I want to show you. You're going to love it."

She shakes her head, and the tenting situation in my pants is finally resolved.

Standing and scooting past me, she ventures to the kitchen. I can see a sliver of her tummy when she reaches into the cabinet for a glass.

"Do you want some water?" she asks with a quick glance at me before her gaze skitters away. The rigid line of her shoulders reveals her feelings even though she hasn't voiced them.

"No, I'm okay," I say as I approach her.

She turns to face me, the kiss-dazed expression on her face gone. I miss it. Instead, her clear brown eyes look back at me. I don't know if there is an actual sheen of tears or if it's a trick of the lighting.

"You're leaving?" she asks. "You're only here for a week?"

I nod. "Yeah. Coming here was a spur-of-the-moment thing. I have assignments lined up for the next six or seven weeks until right before Christmas. I have events in Spain and Portugal for one leg and then Germany and Switzerland back-to-back for the Christmas markets. You'll love the Christmas markets. You have a current passport, right?"

I thought I had seen all of Daphne Foster's expressions, but this mixture of sadness, disappointment, and anger combined is something I never expected to see on her beautiful face.

"You're here for a week on a spur-of-the-moment whim and think I can drop everything to go off with you when you leave? Logan, I have a job. I have responsibilities. I can't wake up and decide to go off on a lark because you drop in, ask me to be yours, then say

'Hey, let's go to Portugal!' *My* life doesn't work like that. I don't know what made you think I'd go for it."

She takes a deep breath. Okay, that sheen isn't from the lighting. It's tears. Now the question is, are they sad tears or angry tears? I guess they could be both? We've never fought before, and I'm not sure we're fighting now, but whatever this is, it's the closest to fighting we've ever gotten. And if I don't figure out what to say, we'll be fighting for sure. Even my bird brain knows that saying her job doesn't need her isn't the right way to go. She hates her job. If they called her tomorrow and said they closed her department and no longer needed her, I bet she'd be thrilled.

Hmm...would Dad and Uncle Will go along with that? Who am I kidding? She'd freak out about not having a job, especially if it was a sudden thing.

Okay, think, Morris. You can do this.

Daphne's pacing, restless. She throws her hands up in the air. "Up and follow you across the world? I can't do that. I want to be with you. I care about you. But I need to work, Logan. Yeah, I have my trust fund, but that can't be the only income that supports us. We'll have to have a home, raise a family, pay for college educations, and fund a retirement. Plus, I need to *do* something. I can't just be stagnant."

"You're right, Daphne. It's not fair for me to spring this on you and think you'll just jump in my arms, ready to run away with me. Let's sit and figure this out." I reach out for her hand, and she doesn't pull away. That's a good sign, right?

She shakes her head. Not a good sign. Crap.

She's still shaking her head, her shoulders slumped. "Logan, it's late. I don't want to talk about this now. I need to get to bed so I'm not a zombie at work tomorrow. Can we discuss it when I get home tomorrow night? It's been a long day, and I'm beat."

I'd rather discuss it now so we can hash it out and move on, but Daphne's tired. She's had a lot sprung on her today. If I push to talk now, she'll dig in her heels, and I won't like the results. Where I'm a face-things-head-on-and-fix-it-all-now type of person, Daphne needs time to process everything and decide on her own. Could I say and do the right things to get her to do what I want eventually? Yeah, probably. But I will not manipulate her. That's an asshole thing to do. This is long-haul stuff, not just a right-now solution.

I pull her toward me and wrap my arms around her waist. I rest my chin on the crown of her head. After a moment, I feel her arms circle around my waist, and she rests her cheek against my chest.

She presses a kiss over my heart and gazes up at me. "I don't want to fight with you."

I give her a gentle squeeze. "Oh, Daph. We aren't fighting. We're figuring out. Let's go to bed, and we'll talk about it tomorrow."

She smiles and stretches up to kiss me. Our lips cling to each other, but we don't deepen the kiss.

She pulls back first and gives me a soft smile. "Okay, you're right. We'll talk about it tomorrow. Good night." With a quick peck, she pulls from my arms and goes to her bedroom.

And closes the door.

I guess I'm sleeping in the other bedroom? Yeah, this was not how I was expecting this night to go. I turn off the TV and the lights in the living room and kitchen, grabbing my pillow and blanket as I go. I'll need them on my lonely bed tonight.

15

DAPHNE

WHAT ARE WE DOING? WHY AM I IN HERE ALONE? I TURN AND OPEN MY door in time to hear the click of Logan's door closing. Okay, I guess I'm in here by myself. Nothing new with that. I'm always alone. I'm always going to be alone. I ease my door closed again. The creak of the bed when Logan sits on it sounds so loud in the quiet house. We share a wall, with our headboards inches apart. It feels like a million miles separating us, not just a few two-by-fours and drywall. I climb into bed and make sure I set the alarm on my phone. Normally, I'd play an audiobook or one of my favorite music playlists as I drift off to sleep, but Logan will hear what I play, and I don't want to keep him awake. No reason for us both to be awake all night.

I stare up at the ceiling. What a day. So much has happened. Never in a million years when I set off this morning to visit the remaining lighthouses did I expect to see Logan and have him tell me he wants to be with me. Or to spend the night cuddling and kissing him. Or for him to ask me to pick up and go to Europe. It hasn't even been eight hours since we met at the Cape May Lighthouse. How has my life changed so much in such a short time span?

Of course, isn't that the way it happens with me? My life gets upended in a moment, and then I have to deal with it. At least this time it isn't a loss. This is a good thing. Right?

Yes, this is a wonderful thing. He says he cares about me and wants to be together. He's here for a week, and then he's gone again until December. We'll be apart more than we are together. Is the plan that we'll be friends with benefits when we're on the same continent and only friends when we're apart? Is this one week together the start of something long-term or just an experiment? If I only get him for a week, I'll take it, but I need to protect myself. No being swept away. No sex. No *I love you*. My world won't be destroyed when he leaves me. This time I'm going to be prepared. I couldn't prepare for a drunk driver leaving me an orphan, but I can prepare for Logan to break my heart. It will hurt, but it'll be worth it to experience being the one he wants, even for a few days.

I roll to my side and punch my pillow to get it right. I settle my head and sigh.

I whisper, "Goodnight, Logan."

Logan's voice drifts through the drywall. "Goodnight, Daph. Sleep well, sweetheart."

His words thrill me even when whispered through a wall, and I smile into my pillow, pressing my hand flat against the headboard as if I can reach him that way.

This needs to be okay. I'm not sure I can handle it if it's not.

Fumbling to shut off my alarm before it wakes Logan next door, I'm shocked I fell asleep. I thought for sure sleep would elude me. I toss back the covers and head to the connected bathroom. I take the time to shave my legs and other areas now that there's a chance someone is going to see them. I don't go full-on Chewbacca—not that there's anything wrong with that—but I don't shave every single day. My stomach growls, but I take my time getting ready. I'm not worried about setting fashion trends, but for the first time, I dread facing Logan.

Okay, time to be brave. I grab my purse and phone. The delicious scents of breakfast cooking greet me as I open my bedroom door. I wasn't expecting Logan to be up this early, but I guess it makes sense he's awake. His body clock most likely hasn't adjusted to East Coast time yet. It would be early afternoon in Europe now, and he'd be up and working unless he had a night shoot the prior evening.

I follow the scents of bacon and coffee into the kitchen. The coffee is for him. I'm a tea drinker, but I hope there's bacon for me. I take a moment to appreciate the sight of a sleep-rumpled Logan standing at my stove in his T-shirt and flannel pants. He's barefoot. It's crazy, but the casualness of him being barefoot and the domesticity of him cooking for me makes my tummy flutter. And not from hunger. Well, not hunger for food.

"Hey, sunshine. I was about to knock on your door." Logan leans in to give me a sweet kiss as I sidle up next to him at the stove, where he's scrambling eggs with ham and shredded cheese. "I don't think I've seen you in yellow before. You're so pretty. Like a cheery ray of sunshine."

I put four slices of bread in the toaster to accessorize our eggs and bacon. "I love this color, but it's not the best color for me to wear. I saw it in the store on sale and thought *screw it* and bought it, anyway." I shrug. "It makes me happy, and I decided that's good enough."

"Well, to me, you're beautiful no matter what you wear. All I want is for you to be happy, so say screw it all you want. I'm quite the fan of screwing, actually." An exaggerated, lascivious wink accompanies that statement.

I plate the toast and walk to the breakfast bar, shaking my head and blushing. "You're ridiculous, you know that, right?" I set the toast on the counter and rummage in the fridge for the grape jelly

Logan likes on his toast. I grab another butter knife from the drawer. We need separate knives for the butter and the jelly—we aren't barbarians. The rest of the silverware is already at our seats. He carries the plates holding our bacon and eggs to the counter and slides into the seat next to mine. My tea is just how I like it and the perfect temperature. I take a bite of the expertly cooked bacon and moan.

I rest my head against his bicep and sigh. "I could get used to this. I usually heat up a couple of waffles or get a toasted bagel from Wawa if I have to stop for gas. This is quite the treat."

"Woman can't live on carbs alone, Daph. You need protein too. You're probably hungry by ten and ravenous by lunch." Logan appears distressed at my lack of a balanced breakfast.

I won't tell him about hitting the stash of pretzel rods in the break room around a quarter past ten to help me make it to lunch. I'll keep my desk stash of granola bars a secret too.

"Yes, dear. You're right," I say instead. "Thank goodness you're here to care for me today." I take a bite of my delicious eggs. The flavors of ham and cheddar make my taste buds tingle. I could get used to this, but I know I can't. He's only here for a week, and then he's off again for however long. I won't dwell on that now. I'm going to enjoy the fact we're together for breakfast.

I glance at him. "What's your plan for today?"

Swallowing his sip of coffee, Logan replies, "Do laundry. If you have anything you need washed, let me know. I can do it with mine."

I shake my head.

"While laundry is going, I figured I'd clean out the gutters, rake the yard. Then I'll grab a shower and meet my gorgeous girlfriend for lunch." He bats his eyelashes. He has the prettiest eyelashes, it's not fair.

I nod. "Yes, please."

"After that, assuming I can't convince her to play hooky for the afternoon..." He casts me a hopeful puppy dog look.

I shake my head again. "Not a chance."

His shoulders droop in resignation. "After that, I'll swing by Uncle Will's office and check in."

"Sounds like a plan," I say. "Oh, that reminds me! I saw Liam the other day. He was doing some minor maintenance stuff in my area of the building. You should call him while you're here. Maybe you can get together. He invited me out with his friends, but I was doing the challenge."

"Do you hang out with Liam a lot?"

"No, I don't hang out with anyone other than Jessica Fletcher. And now Shelby from college. You know that!" What a weird question. Why would he care if I hang out with Liam?

"We'll all have to go out. Maybe go to the casino. We haven't done that in forever. Maybe Devil's Den?" He names one of the newer Atlantic City casinos. It's smaller and more like an old-fashioned gambling club in nineteenth-century England than a neon wonderland.

I haven't been there yet. I'm not much of a gambler. They do have lounges and restaurants besides the gaming, from what I've heard, so maybe it will be fun.

I stand and take my dishes to the sink to rinse them off. "That sounds good. Maybe Friday or Saturday? Talk to Liam and let me know." I take Logan's dishes from his hand and rinse them while he takes mine to load the dishwasher. He has *opinions* on the proper way to load it, so I let him have his fun. I don't care as long as I have clean dishes when I need them.

Turning away from the sink, I lean over to kiss Logan goodbye. "Thank you for breakfast. It was delicious. I have lunch at one this week. Where do you want to go?"

"It's nice out. I could snag sandwiches and chips, and we could go to the park," Logan suggests, resting his hand on my hip.

I look up into the face I love so much. His eyes are such a gorgeous forest green. There are flecks of gold in there if you look closely enough. I love being close enough to him to see them.

His hand flexes on my hip. "Daph?"

I got so lost gazing at him I forgot to respond. "Sandwiches in the park sound great. Turkey club and red bag Herr's, please. Are we meeting there, or are you picking me up?" I ease back and snag my purse from the back of my stool, checking to make sure my keys are in the pocket. I glance up at him, waiting for an answer.

He nods. "A gentleman picks up his lady for their date. You know that, Daphne." Logan slips his feet into his sneakers near the door. "If you're going to insist on going to work, I'm going to insist on walking you to your car." He holds his hand out for my keys, and I give them to him. He wraps the fingers of his free hand around mine, and we walk outside. I hear the click of the car door unlocking. He pulls it open, handing the keys to me.

Before getting in, I turn, wrap my arms around his neck, and stretch up to give him a kiss goodbye. His arms encircle me in return, and his hands rest right above my butt. Our goodbye kiss deepens. His embrace tightens, and I press myself closer. I can taste his morning coffee on his lips. Usually I don't like coffee, but I could learn to enjoy this. I'm not sure how long our kiss lasts, but the *beep beep* of the yellow school bus rumbling past causes us to break apart.

I laugh a bit breathlessly, hoping I didn't give the school kids too much of a show, and get in my SUV. I peek up at Logan after getting settled.

He's holding my door and has stepped in to press a quick kiss to my lips. "Have a good day, sunshine. I'll be there at one to take you to lunch. If you change your mind about the turkey, text me." He steps back and gets ready to close the door.

I stop him. "I'm so glad you're here, Logan. I can't wait for lunch." With that, I let him close my door. Turning the key in the ignition, I give the car a moment to warm up and plug in my phone so I can listen to my current audiobook on my way to the office.

He stands on the porch, watching me and waving as I blow him a kiss. He catches it and presses it to his heart, causing me to melt at his romantic goofiness. After checking to make sure all is clear behind me, I back down the driveway, giving another little wave before I put the car in drive and head off. If I'm only going to get a handful of these mornings with Logan before he leaves me and we're done, I need to remember every moment.

It's all I'm going to have for the future.

16

LOGAN

"BLARGH." THE GROAN SLIPS OUT WHEN I OPEN MY EMAIL AND SEE THE number of unread messages I must deal with. I scroll to the bottom of my inbox and scroll up, marking the ones I can delete. After that first pass, I'm able to dump about two-thirds of the messages, so that's a relief.

"Hmm...I wonder what Marisol wants?" I click on the message. I met Marisol in Madrid a few years ago, and we spent a few pleasant nights together when I was there on assignment, but we never hooked up. It didn't feel right. My heart was with Daphne. She's happily married now, with a little boy and a baby girl.

To: Logan Morris

From: Marisol Figueroa-Sebastien

Hola, Logan, I hope all is well. We are good. Henri is getting into trouble as only a little boy can. Pierre's mother says he takes after his papa. My little man misses his Tio Logan, so you must come visit soon. You need to meet your honorary niece, Ariana! Any progress with the fair Daphne? I want the chance to spoil your children as much as you spoil mine. I have baby's first castanets waiting for a recipient. ;-) Don't be a stranger! Abrazos, Mari.

Baby's first castanets? That's cold. Henri would have discovered "Baby Shark" eventually, even without my help, and he can sing it in both Spanish and French. My little buddy is the smartest two-year-old ever. I've seen pictures of Ariana. She's a beautiful baby, with Pierre's blond hair and Mari's nose. I will absolutely make time to see them while I'm in Spain.

I imagine what my kids will look like. I'd love to have a little girl with Daphne's brown eyes and a smattering of freckles. I've seen pictures of her parents, and her mom had red hair. So does mine. Maybe we'll end up with a redhead. My mom would love to spoil a little girl since she only had me and my younger brother. She had fun doing "girl stuff" with my cousin Kendall, and she has a secret stash of American Girl doll stuff she thinks we aren't aware of just waiting for a little girl to have tea parties with. She'd have tea parties with little boys too, of course, but without a doubt, Mom and my aunt Faith are both hoping for little girls to spoil in the next generation.

Wow. Kids. Never thought of them before. I always assumed I'd be a father one day, but it was an abstract thought. I can see it with Daphne, though. She'd be a great mom. Does she want kids? She's never talked about getting married or having a family. I assume she'll want kids someday. Not too soon though. We have so many places to go, and it's easier to do that without a kid. I want Daph all to myself. I'm in no rush to share her.

I shoot off a reply to Marisol.

To: Marisol Figueroa-Sebastien

From: Logan Morris

Hey Mari, I'm good. Baby's first castanets? Really? Henri loving being a big brother? Pierre hinting for baby number three yet? I can't wait to meet my beautiful niece, Ariana. She will love her Tio Logan. I'm more charming than either of your brothers. I'll be in Spain for a few weeks in November, so count on me dropping by. As for Daphne...see attached. Hugs to you too. Logan.

I attach the picture of us kissing in front of the Cape May Lighthouse. I can't believe that was less than twenty-four hours ago. It feels like a lifetime has passed since yesterday. I hear the dryer buzz and go to take care of the laundry before I leave for lunch with Daphne.

As I get in my Jeep to pick up lunch, I reflect on how fortunate we are that it's a nice day for October—upper sixties, so not too hot but not cold enough that you don't want to sit in the fresh air. It's going to be a good day for lunch outside, and there's a park with a pond and picnic tables close to Daphne's office.

I pick up the food and arrive in the lobby of her office building five minutes early.

"Logan!"

I turn and see my uncle Will approaching from the elevator bank, his green gaze, so like mine, sparkling.

"Hey, Uncle Will, I was going to come visit you after lunch. Are you heading out or coming back?"

Holding out his hand for a shake, he says, "Heading out. Wish to join me?"

"Thanks, but I'm meeting Daphne, and we're going to the park. Ah, here she comes."

Daphne comes out the door to the right of the elevator bank. I guess her work area is on the ground floor. She sees me and walks toward us, smiling. I reach out my hand, and when she takes it, I pull her into a hug.

"Now I see why you turned me down, Logan. Hello, Daphne." Uncle Will smiles at her. "How are things down here today?"

I'm impressed she keeps a straight face when she responds. "Hi, Will. They're great. We're living the dream!"

"You're full of it, but I appreciate the attempt." He laughs. "Have fun, you two. Logan, come on up when you get back. We'll catch up. Keep holding down the fort, Daphne."

We all smile and nod at each other, and Uncle Will heads out, holding the door for an attractive auburn-haired woman entering.

"Thanks, Will!" she says with a smile.

"Mallory!" Daphne waves the woman over. "Mallory, this is my boyfriend, Logan. Logan, this is Mallory, my cellmate. She keeps me sane. Sane-ish."

The smile on Mallory's face gets even bigger. "Logan! You are one of my most favorite people for putting that smile on Daphne's face! Nice to meet you."

I hold my hand out to shake. Her hand is small but strong. You can tell a lot about a person from their handshake, and I like her immediately.

"Great to meet you too, Mallory," I say. "Thanks for keeping my girl's sanity intact."

Laughing, we part ways with Mallory and head out to the parking lot. I open the passenger door to my Jeep so Daphne can get in. We drive to the park and sit on a bench near the gazebo with a view of the pond. Canada geese and mallards swim along, and a gentle breeze ruffles the multicolored leaves in the trees.

She opens the potato chips—red bag Herr's, per her request—and sets the bag on the bench between us.

I hold out both bottles to her. "Water or Diet Pepsi?"

She decides on water then pulls our sandwiches from the bag. "Tastyklairs! You got dessert? No wonder I let you be my boyfriend."

I gladly accept the kiss she offers and show restraint in keeping it light. She'll have to return to the office, and there are other folks around who don't need a peep show.

Pulling back, I unwrap my hoagie and take a bite. "Oh, how I have missed you."

"You're talking to your hoagie, aren't you?"

I groan at the flavors hitting my tongue. I've been all around the world and had many delicious meals, but the perfect bread of a South Jersey sub is a thing of wonder. They say it's the water, and maybe so, but whatever it is, it's magical.

Daphne laughs at me. "Are you sure you came home for me? I'm pretty sure it was an excuse to get a sub."

"No, it was all you, sweetheart," I assure her. "But I won't pass up the opportunity to have the good stuff!" I consider what I just said. "Yeah, good stuff, but you're the best stuff." Winking, I reach in the bag for a chip. This feels right. We've always teased each other, and we're still doing that, but now we can be free with our affection too. Why did we wait so long to do this?

Daphne's eyes keep darting to me, looking over my body. She's chewing her bottom lip. She does that when she's nervous. I hope she doesn't hurt it. Those lips are for kissing me.

"Um...yesterday was the first time I saw you in eagle form, and I didn't know it was you."

"I wanted to surprise you."

"You did! It was a wonderful surprise. The best." Now she's started twisting her fingers. What is she so worried about? Doesn't she know I'll do anything in my power to make her happy?

She takes a deep breath. "Would you shift for me again sometime? I hope that's not a tacky thing to ask for."

That's what she was so nervous about?

"Sure! I can shift now." The park isn't that busy. If we go on a trail in the woods, I can shift in privacy.

"You can? How? Don't you have to take off your clothes so they don't rip?"

My chuckle tickles as it travels up my throat. "Daph, I'm a shifter, not the Incredible Hulk. Our clothes shift with us. It's some kind of magic. I just need to empty my pockets. I'm smaller shifted than I am as a man, so I'd be a bird wearing a shirt too big for me, looking ridiculous. It's the wolf and bear shifters that would do the dramatic busting out of clothes thing if our clothes didn't shift."

We finish our sandwiches, throw out the trash, and Daphne carries the bag with our pies, leftover chips, and drinks as we take a trail into the woods. We enter a clearing and, after looking around to make sure we have privacy, I take off my sneakers and socks and drop my phone, wallet, and keys on them. Stepping back, I take a deep breath and shift. I'm lucky my shifts aren't that dramatic. I'm able to do it smoothly without lots of cracking and contorting. When Mom or Andy shift, they go from being a biped to being on four legs, and their focus is closer to the ground. I'm still upright, and I have the advantage of having a wider field of vision.

"Wow," Daphne says reverently. "You're gorgeous." She looks at me in awe.

In the past twenty-four hours, I've thought more about how I look in my eagle form than I ever have since I've started shifting as a kid. I've never shifted in front of someone I'm dating before. It's a personal thing and not a party trick. The few shifter girls I've been with understand, and the human girls—the very few that even knew I was a shifter—didn't care. Our dealings weren't that personal. They were hookups. I preen a bit, extending my wings and flying to perch on a nearby fencepost so we're closer to eye to eye.

Daphne has made me watch enough *America's Next Top Model* that I know my angles and how to find my light, so I make sure the fall sun glints off my feathers, and I look like the regal eagle I am and not like an obese chicken.

Daphne approaches me cautiously. She reaches out a hand and then stops, looking me in my eyes. "Can I touch you?"

If I could speak, I'd tell her she can always touch me. I can't, so I incline my head and extend my wing.

She runs a finger along it gently. "So silky. So many beautiful colors."

I'd love nothing more than to spend the afternoon here with my girl showing off this side of me, but she has to go back to the office.

She must realize the same thing because she checks her phone and twists her lips in a funny face. "Time for you to take me back to the office, dude."

I fly back to my shoes and socks and shift back to my man form, grab my phone, keys, and wallet, put them back in my pockets, and put on my shoes and socks.

"I'd much rather be taking you home, sunshine," I murmur, standing and nuzzling her neck.

She pulls away with a giggle. "Nice try."

We walk out of the woods to the parking area.

As she gets in my Jeep, Daphne asks, "Are we having the leftover pizza and salad for dinner?"

"That's what I was figuring, unless you want something else?"

"Nope, that sounds good. I don't feel like cooking or going anywhere."

I can't believe we've been a couple less than twenty-four hours. It feels so natural. We kiss each other goodbye in the car and walk into the building together. I give her hand a squeeze when we part at the elevators.

Daphne points to a door at the end of a short hallway to the right of the elevators. If you didn't know it was there, you'd never notice it. "My area is over here. I'm sure you know this already, but the reception desk is right when you get off the elevator. Betty will direct you to Will's office."

After one last too-brief kiss, I enter the waiting elevator car to go up to Uncle Will's office while Daphne scans her badge to get into her work area.

I approach Betty, Morgan Development's long-time receptionist, with a smile. "Hi, Betty. Looking lovely, as always. I hope your husband appreciates how lucky he is."

She grins cheekily at me. "Hush, you! You've always been such a flirt, but you won't turn my head. Are you here to see your uncle?"

"Ah, Betty, you missed your chance. I'm taken," I say with a wink. "I believe Uncle Will is expecting me."

She calls and confirms he's free and tells me to head on back. I walk along the hallway to his office where his assistant tells me to make my way on in.

"Uncle Will?" No one is behind the desk. I peer around to see if he's on the couch in his sitting area, but he's not.

"Got us coffee," my uncle says from behind me. He hands me a cup. "Sit down and tell me what's up. You know your aunt is going to want all the details. Your mom has already told her you came home to woo Daphne. They've been reading a lot of those historical romances for their book club, so it's wooing this and courting that."

I take a chair in front of his desk, and he takes his place behind the desk. We both know Aunt Faith chose the hunter-green couch and black watch plaid chairs in the sitting area more for their style than for their comfort.

"Yeah, I came home to woo Daphne." I flex my fingers, putting air quotes around the word *woo*. "I decided it was time to tell her how I feel and see where we stand. Luckily, she feels the same way, so we're dating. I guess that's what you call it. We haven't formally defined it, but I know she's the one for me."

"Like, forever?"

"Yeah, she's my mate."

"She's human, right?"

"She is," I affirm, wondering what he's getting at.

"Usually, we only ever marry other shifters."

"You didn't. Aunt Faith is human."

"Right. That's why I'm bringing this up."

Confusion turns to anger. "What are you suggesting, Uncle Will?"

He shrugs. "Marriage is hard, but when it's a mixed marriage, that adds a level of difficulty."

"What the hell are you talking about?"

"Um... Intimacy is different with a human." He blushes and looks down at his coffee.

"I've slept with non-shifter women. It's no different."

"I mean no offense, Logan. I'm trying to give you the benefit of my experience. It's not just the bedroom. What about kids? A human female carrying a shifter's baby isn't always easy, and they aren't always successful. You open yourself up to a lot of heartache. Faith and I lost twins between Liam and Kendall. It broke our hearts and put a strain on our marriage." He clears his throat and looks away, blinking quickly.

"I'm sorry. I didn't know that." My heart hurts for them. I don't want to do anything that would hurt Daphne or our child.

"Yeah, well, you were a baby, and we don't really talk about it. If you're successful, what happens if your child is a shifter? Suddenly you and the child have something she doesn't—a way to communicate, to be, on a level she can't understand. She may feel like an outsider in her own family. That's hard. That's why most of us marry other shifters." Will fidgets in his chair. "With Liam and Kennie both being cougar shifters too, Faith was left behind sometimes. It was hard. She felt left out."

"I appreciate your advice, Uncle Will, but you don't know us."

"Look, I like Daphne," he assures me, "and I'm happy for you. I'm just warning you. When she's disappointed..."

I try to hold back my huff of annoyance. "It's going to be fine. I have a plan."

"You and your plans." He chuckles.

"What's that supposed to mean?" Seriously, why is everyone getting on my case about having plans like it's a bad thing? How are you supposed to get anything done if you don't have a plan?

"Nothing. So, what's your plan? You know there's always a position here for you at Morgan Development. Your photography skills would be useful in marketing. You have a business degree, and law school is always an option," he says around a chuckle.

"No law school. I'll leave next week for assignments in Spain and Portugal. Then I'll be covering the Christmas markets in Germany and Switzerland."

Uncle Will leans forward and rests his forearms on his desk. "You're leaving again? Is Daphne going with you?"

"We're figuring out what we're doing. I don't think she's coming with me, at least not right away." I sigh. "I don't get it. Daphne has always wanted to travel, and I'm giving her the opportunity to travel and share my adventures." I grimace. "She hates her job." I feel the flush rising in my cheeks when I remember who I'm talking to. "Crap. Forget I said that." I take a sip of my coffee, trying to disguise my gaffe. "This brew is excellent. Where do you get your beans?"

"Ask Betty when you leave. She knows all the info."

Maybe he didn't catch it. "Did you know Daphne's grandmother died before her senior year of college and left her a house? She was expecting Daph to sell it and fund her travels. Instead, Daphne is acting like the house is an anchor. She acts like it's imperative she keeps it and stays in it. Forever."

"I'm sorry she hates her job. She's excellent at it."

I guess he caught it.

"I won't fire her just to make your life easier."

I feel guilty even thinking that. "I know. Daphne needs to decide things for herself." I shift in my chair and rest my ankle on my knee. "She's made the choices she did in reaction to loss and feeling adrift. She wants security. Losing her job would cause her so much stress. She needs to decide to make a change, not be forced into it." I shrug. "Of course we can't mess with her career because I want to be with my girlfriend. Being a mature adult sucks sometimes."

"That it does, Logan. If you ask your grandmother, I'm still resisting it."

I blow out a breath to clear out the thoughts I've been worrying about. "I can't help but hope she decides she wants to come with me."

"What if she never wants to go with you? Being a nomad doesn't suit everyone. Can you put down roots for her? Have you discussed it?"

Trust my uncle to get to the heart of the matter. "We've been a couple less than twenty-four hours. Let us enjoy ourselves, huh?"

He leans back in his chair and sips his coffee. "By all means, enjoy yourselves. But you know these are things you'll have to discuss and work out if you're going to have the long-term relationship I assume you're hoping for." He places his cup on his desk. Aunt Faith insisted he have a coaster. I'll have to tell her he uses it. "I've seen the two of you together over the years. Even if the romantic aspect of your relationship is new, it's obviously not casual. I don't want either of you to get hurt."

I hate it when he's right. "I know. Let's change the subject. Daphne said Liam was doing maintenance here. What's up with that?"

"We're considering a large local project, so he was checking into some preliminary matters. Can't say anything yet, but if it happens, it will be cool." He kicks his feet up on this desk. Aunt Faith wouldn't like that, but I won't tell. "He took care of replacing some lightbulbs and incidental things like that. He'll head out of town in a couple of weeks to visit our southern division properties. He spends a fair amount of time on the road. Not as much as you though."

Chuckling, I stand and hold out my hand for a shake. "I need to call him and see about hanging out while we're both in town. I guess I should let you get back to work. I need to go home and do a bit of editing."

Rising from his desk chair, Uncle Will comes around his desk, takes my hand, and pulls me in for a hug and a slap on the back. "It was so good seeing you, Logan. You're staying at Daphne's, right? The two of you need to come over for dinner before you go. We can invite your parents, Kendall, and Liam, too. It's a shame Andy is away at school or else we'd have the whole family."

"Text me what you have in mind, and I'll run it past Daphne. Even if we don't do dinner, I'll swing by to see Aunt Faith before I go, so she doesn't disown me."

"Sounds good, buddy." He gazes at me steadily. "I'm happy for you. Don't screw it up." With that, Uncle Will retreats behind his desk, and I take my leave.

I wish my conversation with Uncle Will left me feeling better than I do. But I'm walking too fast and clenching my fists. He's *wrong*. Everything will be perfect with Daphne. As long as I can convince her to step out of her old life and into a new one with me.

17
DAPHNE

"Hi, honey, I'm home!" I've always wanted to call that out and have someone there to answer.

Logan comes out from the bedroom we use as an office and wraps me in his arms.

"Hey, sunshine," he says, lowering his head for the kiss my smiling lips offer. "How was your afternoon?"

This feels so nice. It's only been a day since he surprised me at the lighthouse, but it feels so natural. He's leaving in a week and then I'll be alone again, coming home to an empty house. It's going to hurt even more because now I know what I'll be missing. But I won't let those thoughts steal today's joy.

Logan releases me from his embrace but takes my hand to lead me to the breakfast bar where two glasses of iced tea await. I hang my purse from the back of the stool he's pulled out for me and take the glass closest to my spot.

I take a sip. It's cold and deliciously sweet. "Yeah, it's simply water, tea bags, and sugar, no secret ingredients or magic, but somehow you make the best iced tea."

"You think it tastes good because you didn't have to make it."

He's not wrong.

"Ready for dinner?"

Logan pulls a loaf of Italian bread from the counter. "Yeah, I picked up bread too. Do you want me to heat it?"

"Ooh, I love warm Italian bread. I normally nuke it, but if you can throw it in the oven, that would be divine. What did you want to do after dinner? If we aren't going anywhere, I'm going to change."

Logan is turning the oven on to preheat, so I walk over and wrap my arms around his waist from behind. I rest my cheek against his broad back because I can. I never thought I'd be able to touch him like this so freely. It's addicting. Logan turns and wraps his arms around me, resting his hands low on my back.

"I'm good with a night at home," he says in his deep, rumbly voice, causing shivers to run along my spine. He sounds very sexy tonight. "Change into something comfortable. Do you want salad and bread first and then pizza? I'll put a couple slices in to heat when I take the bread out."

"Ooh, aren't you the fancy one?" I can't help but tease him. "We're going to have our leftovers in courses?"

His fingers attack my ribs, tickling.

I double over. "Ack, Logan! Stop!" I twist out of his arms and hustle away from him.

"Just for that, my dear, you will not get the dessert course." Logan thinks he's winning.

He's not. I see the container from the Half-Cocked Bake Shop on the counter. No way is he going to deny me my ultimate chocolate cupcake. Two can play this game.

"Okay, neither of us will get *dessert* tonight." I do the air quote fingers when I toss that statement over my shoulder while walking toward the bedroom. "I have Hallmark movies on the DVR I want to watch."

Logan growls behind me.

I giggle, knowing I'm getting to him. Wiggling my hips, I saunter to my bedroom. I want to wash my face and redo my ponytail. He growls a second time, this one lower and somehow more sensual, telling me he appreciates the show. I change into a T-shirt I just bought representing my favorite baseball team and a pair of yoga pants. I want to be comfortable and normal. Things don't have to change just because we're a couple now.

Right. Sure. Keep telling yourself that, Daphne.

Instead of going directly back to the living room, I pop into the other bedroom and snag Logan's pillows and put them in my room. In our room, I guess. I want to spend the night in his arms every night possible. I'm an idiot for getting cold feet last night and missing the opportunity. I blame my shock over finally taking our relationship to a romantic level. I'm not making that mistake again!

I watch Logan's back muscles flex as he pulls the warm bread from the oven when I reenter the dining area. My mouth waters, and not just from the homey, yeasty scent wafting from the loaf. I could get used to having someone here when I come home and not having to deal with eating dinner alone every night.

He turns and laughs at my shirt featuring a baseball-playing mallard duck. "Cute shirt. It's new, right? I'm heating two slices for me. How many do you want?"

I grab the breadboard and knife to slice the bread. "Thanks. Yeah, it's new." I stick my tongue out at him. "I buy my own T-shirts once in a while. I don't have to steal them from you. I just like to." Logan wraps his hand in my ponytail and guides my lips to his for a searing kiss.

"Daphne, if you're going to stick your tongue out at me, you better plan on using it," he says with a smirk.

I blink at him dazedly. He asked me a question, but I can't remember what it was. I look around. Pizza. He asked about pizza.

"One slice of plain is good. Need to save room for my cupcake," I reply, winking. My wink inspires the eye roll I was expecting. "Did you get one for yourself too? I don't want you to miss out on dessert."

He responds by placing the salad bowl and plates on the dining room table and turning to grab silverware from the drawer. I follow with the sliced bread and butter dish.

After dinner, we sit on the couch eating our cupcakes. Ultimate chocolate for me, and carrot cake for Logan. I swear he picks that because he knows I won't poach it. It's got raisins. Gross. I flip through my recordings on the DVR, knowing he'll watch a Howlbark Channel movie with me. He's done it dozens of times before, even though it's not his favorite thing. They're sappy romance movies with a shifter twist. I've watched all the human movies with the big city girl returning to her small town and reconnecting with her former love. These are mostly the same but the flannel-wearing hometown sweetheart may be a wolf shifter with a love of the outdoors and their conflict is she's a cougar shifter whose idea of roughing it is drinking coffee brewed at home.

"What do you want to watch?" I look over to see him licking the cream cheese frosting off his top lip. I've never been envious of cream cheese before. Great, I can feel my cheeks heat, the curse of being fair-skinned—I can't hide my blushes.

"Are you okay? You appear flushed." Logan reaches over to feel my forehead. "Do you think you have a fever?" He tilts his head and narrows his gaze. "Your forehead is cool. Hmm...were you thinking naughty thoughts about me?" He runs his tongue slowly over his upper lip.

That jerk. He knows exactly why my face is flushed!

Just for that, we're watching a marathon of Howlbark mystery movies. Who wouldn't love watching actresses from favorite shows of the 90s solve murders while baking/matchmaking/walking dogs/spelunking? Okay, no spelunking yet, but it's a matter of time. Who am I kidding? I'm not planning on actually watching the movie I've selected.

I have a boyfriend to cuddle with!

18

LOGAN

THANK GOODNESS DAPHNE WASN'T PLANNING ON WATCHING THE MOVIE. She's too darn kissable to resist.

"I can't get enough of kissing you," I breathe against her lips. I can't believe I have to leave so soon. The knowledge fills me with urgency, longing, sadness. I kiss her harder, not wanting to let go, not now that I've got what I want after all this time. How will I be able to leave her behind? But I must. I'm committed until right before Christmas. But then I'll be home, and we can figure out what to do next.

"I can't get enough of being kissed," Daphne murmurs, raining kisses along my jawline before snuggling against my side to continue watching the movie.

An hour later, I whisper, "Are you ready to call it a night? You need to get up early for work tomorrow." I place a kiss against her crown.

I could spend countless nights here cuddling on the couch. I love holding her in my arms. If we could sleep here so I didn't have to release her, I would, but she has to go to work in the morning, and this couch wasn't designed for two people to sleep comfortably on.

Okay, it's not meant for one person of my size to sleep comfortably on, but I'd suffer if it meant Daphne was in my arms all night.

When she sits up, I lean to press a kiss where her shoulder meets her neck. She shivers oh-so-slightly. I love how responsive she is to my touch.

"Yeah, I guess so," she says. "I was so comfy I was about to doze off. I love snuggling with you. You give good cuddles." She stretches and wiggles to turn around and face me.

I'm thinking of creepy clown puppets in an attempt to keep my cock calm in my black basketball shorts. He's been perking up in interest all night long, but I don't need him at full attention and waving hello like he's the Queen of England in a parade.

She kisses my chin and moves to put her feet on the floor and stand. I want to pull her back against me, but that will lead to a lot more cuddling and kissing with no sleeping. She gathers our cupcake papers and other snack trash and walks to the kitchen to take care of it. I check the locks on the doors and start turning off lights as we make our way back to the bedrooms. Daphne goes into her room, and I enter the hallway bathroom to brush my teeth.

"Where are you going?" Daphne asks, standing in her doorway. She's ditched the yoga pants and is wearing only her oversized T-shirt and showing miles of shapely legs.

I feel like this is a trick question. "To bed?" As far as I know, that's the right answer.

She smiles. "I moved your pillows in here. Is that okay?"

"Hell yes!" I picture myself resembling the cartoon Road Runner with my legs spinning in a circle in my rush to get into her bedroom. It's not a very sexy look for me, but it makes my girl giggle, so it's all good. We've shared beds before when we've fallen asleep watching TV or stayed over somewhere after a night out with limited sleeping spots. "Let me brush my teeth and I'll be in," I say, closing the bathroom door.

With my teeth freshly brushed, I join Daphne in her bedroom. It's a pretty room with white furniture we bought at IKEA and spent an afternoon putting it together while reading the instructions in our version of Swedish accents. We sounded more like the Muppet chef than anyone human, but it was fun. Her queen-size bed has a green and purple floral quilt on it that her Gran made. Gran was a prolific quilter, and I'm pretty sure she has baby quilts packed away for Daphne's future children. Our future children, I hope.

"You still sleep on the right side? That's where I put your pillows, but we can switch..." She's worrying her lower lip as if she's nervous. Ah, my sweet girl.

"Right side is perfect. I'm honestly good with whatever." I see my phone and charger on the nightstand, plugged in on that side already, and there's a bottle of water. The only thing missing is a mint on the pillow. I walk over and turn down the covers on my side of the bed, and then stop. I normally sleep nude, but I can't do that tonight. When we've shared a bed before, we fell asleep wearing what we wore. It wasn't a pre-planned thing.

Daphne notices my hesitation. "What's up? If you don't want to sleep in here, that's okay." No, that's not okay. I want to spend as many nights by her side as possible. There's nowhere else I want to be.

"Of course I want to be in here." I feel the blush color my cheeks. I'm a grown man, and I'm blushing like that time I walked in on my parents. "I was trying to figure out what to wear."

Daphne shrugs. "Wear what you normally wear."

"I don't normally wear anything, honey."

Now it's Daph's turn to blush. "Oh! Um...okay..."

I laugh softly. "No, I'm good. I'll take off my shirt and leave my shorts on, okay?"

She nods.

"Daphne." I wait for her eyes to meet mine across the bed. "We're just sleeping. It's okay. We can cuddle. I'd love to hold you throughout the night, but nothing more is going to happen until you're ready for it. Until we're both ready for it. And we're not ready yet. We have forever. There's no rush."

The smile she gives me is shy but glorious. I want her to always give me that smile in our bedroom.

I open my mouth to tell her I love her but close it quickly. Too soon. Still too soon. How long will I have to swallow how I feel, silence it?

"Is something wrong?" she asks, climbing into the bed.

"No. Nothing." I follow her lead, and thankfully find something to distract her. And me.

"You're using the blue cartoon moose sheets I bought you last Christmas. I never thought

I'd have the chance to sleep on them." I turn off the lamp on my side of the queen-size bed, enjoying the softness of the flannel sheets against my skin.

Daphne turns off her lamp, and we lie side by side on our backs in the dark. Her giggles fill the room, and my deep chuckle joins in. I reach over and clasp her hand.

"Why is this so awkward?" she asks. "We've slept together before."

I scoot toward her as she's scooting toward me. We meet in the middle, our bodies instinctively knowing how best to cuddle together. I grab her hand and lift it to my lips to press a gentle kiss to her palm, then I lower it to rest over my heart, my hand covering hers. We lie like this for a few minutes when I feel her wiggle a bit.

"What do I do with my other arm?" Her question breaks the silence. She moves, trying to figure out what to do. I love her awkward self. Our life will never be boring. "I like the way we're cuddling, but I don't know what to do with this arm. None of my romance novels ever mention what to do with the bottom arm. Do they pretend it doesn't exist, or does everyone else know what to do with it but me?"

I can't help it. I laugh. She's adorable. "Do whatever you want with your arm. You could lay more on your stomach and have it stretched out on the other side or lay more on your back so it's not under you. Tuck it up under your cheek. We could spoon."

She's tensing. This is upsetting her. She hates it when she doesn't know what to do. Uncertainty makes her nervous. I stop laughing. It's not funny if she's stressed.

"You could lie however you usually do. We don't have to cuddle. I know you need to get up for work in the morning. Do whatever you need to do so you can sleep." I hope she doesn't take that last option. I want to hold her.

Daph gets up from the bed, does a full-body shimmy that causes her breasts to jiggle—I'm a fan of that move—and resumes her spot under the covers. She lies on her side against me, but this time her lower arm is bent with her hand under her chin, so her arm isn't trapped between us. She rests her head against my chest again, and lays her hand over my heart.

I cover her hand with mine and kiss the crown of her head. "All good now?"

Her contented sigh blows across my chest, causing goosebumps to rise along my skin.

"All good. Goodnight." She presses a kiss to my chest.

"Goodnight, sweetheart."

Holding Daphne like this is something I've dreamed of but didn't dare think about too much. I didn't think it would happen, but here we are. I can sense when she's drifted off to sleep—her whole body relaxes, and her breathing deepens. She'll deny it with her last breath, but she snores slightly. It's adorable. I enjoy the luxury of being here and holding her until I drift off to sleep myself.

19

DAPHNE

I REACH TOWARD THE NIGHTSTAND TO SILENCE THE TRILLING OF MY PHONE'S alarm. Morning has come way too soon. It's not fair. Logan is the big spoon to my little spoon. Waking with him warm against my back, his arm snug around my waist and his morning hardness snug against my rear, is as wonderful as I always imagined it to be. Okay, the hard-on against my butt is a bit more than I expected... Wowsers... Focus, Daphne. I want to wake up every morning in Logan's arms. How am I going to sleep alone again when he leaves next week?

"Hmm...Good morning, baby." Logan's arm tightens around me, and he places a soft kiss on the back of my neck. I shiver deliciously, my heart speeding up at his gentle touch. I turn around to face him. We stare at each other and burst out laughing. Oh, my goodness, the morning breath we have! We roll to our backs and hold hands as our laughter subsides.

"Daphne." Logan turns his head to smile at me. "I love waking up next to you, but you need a breath mint."

"*I* need a breath mint?" I glance over at him. His morning stubble is so sexy. "Dude, you have Chernobyl breath yourself. You're going to save me time getting ready. You just need to breathe on me, and my hair will curl."

The bed bounces from his renewed laughter. "So, what you're saying is if we want to have morning cuddles, we need to keep TicTacs on our nightstands?" Logan's deep chuckles are such a wonderful soundtrack to my morning. I'm used to waking up alone in the silence. I turn on the TV to have noise and the illusion of company while I get ready for work. Having someone here with me, not being alone, is wonderful. I don't think I realized how lonely I've been until I had Logan here again. He's only been here two days, and already I can't imagine coming home to an empty house after work and starting my day in silence. I'm going to have to prepare myself for his departure.

"Hey, what are you thinking? You got serious over there." Logan rolls to his side and brushes my hair off my face. He must be able to see inside my head because his face loses its earlier mirth, and his forest-green gaze seems to darken. "Daph, stop. You're thinking about me leaving next week." He takes a deep breath. "Baby, it will be okay. Don't ruin the time we have together now, stressing over the time we'll be apart."

He's right, but it's hard. I want him to stay here with me. I attempt a smile, but it's feeble. I hate this. I finally have him here with me, and I'm already counting down the days until he leaves again. I can't enjoy our time together because I'm expecting the end. I'm so tired of people leaving me. I'm so tired of being left behind. I know my parents and Gran didn't leave me by choice. Logan is choosing to leave though.

"I think I hate when you know what I'm thinking. I can't have any secrets." I roll away from him and get out of bed. "I'll start your coffee brewing. What do you want to do for breakfast? I don't think we have a lot of eggs left, so no full breakfast like you spoiled me with yesterday."

Logan throws back the covers and rises from the bed. I can't help but stare at his broad chest and feel giddy that I had the luxury of

using it for my pillow last night. My gaze travels down over his abs—
tight and bisected by his happy trail, leading to his... My gaze flies
back up to his face, and he smirks. That jerk knows me too well.

"I remember you had bagels in the freezer, so I could fry us each
an egg, put it on a toasted bagel with cheese, and voilà—homemade
Sizzli sandwich." He walks toward the door to the hallway. "I'll take
care of my Godzilla breath and start breakfast. You do your thing."
He checks out the clock on the dresser. "Breakfast in thirty sound
good? That enough time for you?"

I nod and watch him leave the room. Leave our bedroom. Holy
cow. We slept together last night. I sink down on the mattress and
flop back, my arms stretched out to the sides. I spent the night in
Logan Morris's arms, and it was glorious!

I must have let out a little squee of joy because Logan's head
appears in the doorway, and he grins. "I'm all for spending the day in
bed with you, Daph. Say the word. But if you're going to insist on
going to the office, you need to get your cute butt up and get ready."

I groan. "I'm moving. Let me have my moment here. Be a
wonderful boyfriend and prepare sustenance." I flail my hand in my
approximation of a royal wave to send him on his way. I can hear his
chuckle as he moves down the hall. I could get used to this.

20

LOGAN

WE'RE SITTING IN MY JEEP AT A STOPLIGHT, ON OUR WAY TO MY UNCLE'S house, and Daphne looks like she's about to hurl. She's pale and tapping her fingers on her thigh.

I reach over and grab her hand, stroking it, trying to calm her. "Why are you nervous? You know everyone that's going to be there. They all adore you. I'm pretty sure some of them like you more than they like me."

Giving my hand a squeeze, Daphne grins. "Just your dad. Your mom still likes you best."

"Sunshine, you've charmed all the men in my family. Uncle Will and Liam are big fans of yours, and I'm pretty sure Andy had a crush on you. You were the alluring older college woman, so much more worldly than the girls in his freshman high school class."

Her giggle is like a crystal bell. "Yeah, I was so alluring in my hoodies and Chucks. You couldn't even tell I had boobs!"

I laugh. "Maybe that was the attraction. He *is* gay."

I stop at the red light and gaze at her. She's lovely in her red V-neck sweater that drapes over her breasts enticingly. There's no hiding the fact she has boobs now. Her rich chestnut hair is down around her shoulders in large, loose curls. Big brown eyes meet mine through the lenses of her wire-rimmed glasses.

"What?" she asks.

I smile at her and then turn back to realize the light turned green. "You don't know how lovely you are. It's not what you wear or your boobs. Just so you know, I'm a big fan of your boobs, but that's one—okay, two—of the things that make you captivating. It's so much more than what's on the outside, and you don't see what the rest of us see beyond your beauty. Hey! No scoffing."

Knowing Daphne, she's rolling her eyes in concert with her scoff because she can't take a compliment.

"You *are* beautiful," I insist. "But you're so much more. You're smart and strong and loving and funny. You're the total package... plus a nice rack."

She pulls her hand from my grasp and punches me in the arm.

"Hey! And you have a good jab."

I turn onto my aunt and uncle's street and follow the cul-de-sac to pull up to the curb in front of their house.

"My parents are here. Kendall and Liam too."

My cousin Kennie is home from school for the weekend, and Liam stays in the pool house when he's not traveling on Morgan Development business.

"Yeah, Kennie texted to see what I was wearing. She's so excited to be going to Devil's Den with us after dinner. Says it's the first time she's going to a casino...legally."

Daphne and I shake our heads in tandem. My younger cousin is a spitfire. I turn off the car and lean toward Daphne, placing a gentle kiss on her lips. I could stay like this all night, but I suspect Mom and Aunt Faith are watching. If we linger too long, they'll come out to get us.

Parting reluctantly, I reach in the back seat to grab the box holding the caramel apple cake Daph picked up from the Half-

Cocked Bake Shop on the way home. Daphne takes the cake box from my hands.

"Here, give me the cake. I'll carry it. I know you're going to be subjected to hugs and handshakes the second we walk in. You need your hands free."

"True. I'm surprised we haven't had visitors showing up on the doorstep. I didn't expect them to wait patiently until Friday for us to meet for dinner." I walk around the car to open the door for her. Sure, it's old-fashioned, but I enjoy doing these little things for Daphne. My dad still does these things for Mom, and I see how happy it makes her. I'm fortunate to have them as an example. I would love to have a marriage as strong and happy as my parents. And I want it to be with Daphne. I'm trying to ignore the warning Uncle Will gave me. We're going to be fine.

I love this house. It's a large brick home in an upscale neighborhood, but where other homes on the street are like soulless McMansions, Aunt Faith has infused warmth and character with the potted mums flanking the porch and scarecrows sitting on hay bales on the lawn.

The oak front door opens as we follow the walkway to the porch, and I can see my cousin Kendall waiting for us.

"Finally!" she says. "I thought you guys were going to stay in the car kissing all night and starve me to death."

Kennie is petite and seems delicate, but her years as a competitive cheerleader have given her the metabolism of a linebacker, and she's always hungry. You wouldn't think a five-foot, two-inch pixie could pack away pizza and wings the way she does, but she's a force of nature.

Kennie waves us in. "Mom made her beef stew, and it smells so good. Hurry and get in here so we can get started."

"Kendall Maureen Morgan, go finish setting the table." Aunt Faith appears next to Kennie and snaps her hip with the dishtowel in her hand.

"*Ooh*, you got middle named!" Liam calls out from the living room.

"William James Morgan III. Go help your sister!" Aunt Faith isn't one to take any sass. Years of teaching high school have made her tough. It doesn't matter that her kids are twenty-one and twenty-seven and no longer teenagers. She's in charge, and that's it. I hear Ken tease Liam about being thirded. They are such goofs.

Aunt Faith smiles brightly. "Logan, Daphne! Welcome! Give me a hug." She envelops me in a tight hug. She's like Kendall, tiny but strong.

Uncle Will welcomes Daphne, taking the cake box from her with a smile. "Come on in, guys. Does this need to be refrigerated, Daphne?"

"No, it doesn't have to be. It's a caramel apple cake with cream cheese frosting, so on the slim chance there are leftovers, refrigerate them, but for dessert, it's best to let it come to room temperature while we eat dinner."

We wander further into the house. Dad is pouring wine and gestures toward us with the bottle. I shake my head no since I'm driving, but Daphne smiles and nods yes. I'm assuming my parents brought the wine, so it's probably a Cabernet Sauvignon from a local winery. Mom loves the Cabs.

"About time you two got here!" Mom embraces Daphne and smiles at me over her shoulder. "We were going to start without you!"

"Don't lie, Holly. You were two minutes from calling them." Dad holds out his hand for a shake and pulls me into a backslapping hug. As if they choreographed it, Mom and Dad switch, and I'm getting a hug and cheek kiss from my mother while Dad embraces Daphne. They saw me last Friday, but you'd think it's been two years from the way they're acting.

"Daphne, it's great to see you outside of your dungeon of an office. Will, we need to move Daphne and Mallory upstairs to join the rest of the legal team," Dad says.

Uncle Will turns from setting the cake box on the counter and ambles over to join us, picking up Daph's wine glass and handing it to her.

She takes a big sip.

"You do a great job," Dad continues, "but it's a shame to have you down there. Move you two upstairs where there are windows and natural light. You'd adapt to leasing, or with your accounting background, maybe you'd rather be in finance."

I see the panic on Daphne's face. Work is the last thing she wants to discuss at dinner, or any time, but especially not now.

I clear my throat. "No Morgan Development talk tonight. There's enough to discuss without boring office stuff." Winking at Daphne, I introduce a new subject while we take our seats at the table. "How about the Flyers last night? That power play in the second period was insane, right?" That's the trick to get the conversation on a new track. Everyone except for Mom and Kendall loves hockey and will talk about it anytime, anywhere. Kennie and Mom are similarly rabid over the Phillies, but their season is over. Liam takes the seat on Daphne's other side and gives her a side hug and kiss on the cheek, shooting me a smug look over her head as he pulls away. My parents sit across from us, with Kennie across from Liam. Uncle Will and Aunt Faith are at either end.

We all bend our heads as Aunt Faith says grace. After the 'Amen,' the bowls of stew get passed around from one direction and the basket of warm French bread from the other way. It's a well-choreographed dance from all the family dinners we've had through the years. Since I'm foregoing wine, I only have water with my stew. It is so flavorful nothing else sounds good with it. I know the Cabernet the others are drinking is an excellent wine, but I'm driving us to the casino after dinner and I don't drink at all if I'm driving. Daphne has never said anything, but knowing a drunk driver killed her parents, I don't want her to worry for a second about me driving while impaired.

"This is so good, Faith. Thanks for having us," Daphne says after we've all started eating.

"My pleasure," Aunt Faith replies. "I'm so glad you could visit before Logan heads out again. You leave Monday?"

Grr... I don't want this to be our topic of conversation. She tries to hide it, but I can tell it distresses Daphne to think about me leaving. We discussed it this week, and there were tears, more hers than mine, but I had a few too. We just got together. We're just getting used to being together. As more than friends. It sucks. It may even suck ass.

Daphne has issues about being left behind, and I hate that, but she could always come with me. I'm not leaving her behind. She's choosing to stay here. I have commitments until right before Christmas. Maybe I should have waited until I fulfilled my commitments before coming home and telling Daph about my feelings, but I didn't want to hold back any longer, especially with Liam sniffing around.

I'm not proud to admit that part of it was waiting to make sure she knew how I felt because I was afraid she'd find someone else as part of her mission to go out more. Once she was out, other men would flock to her. I want to make sure she's mine. If Liam was successful in getting Daphne to go out with him, I'm not sure my friendship with him would survive. I couldn't spend holiday dinners across the table from them without wanting to leap across and beat the hell out of Liam. If I saw Daphne kissing him, I'd lose it.

Swallowing my bite of buttered bread, I nod. "Yeah, I leave early Monday evening, arriving in Spain on Tuesday morning. I'll be going to a kite festival on one of the Canary Islands and then the Portugal Horse Fair. I'll be covering the Christmas markets and whatever else I come across. I'll be back the week before Christmas."

Daphne stiffens next to me, and I place my hand on her thigh and give a gentle squeeze. She relaxes slightly, but I know she doesn't like this topic.

Kennie's face lights up, and she gives a slight squee. "Ooh, that's exciting! Will this be your first time going, Daphne?"

Ah, damn. Why did Kendall have to bring that up? An awkward silence falls around the table. Apparently, no one filled in Kennie regarding the situation.

Liam refills Daphne's wine, and she picks up the glass as she answers. "I'm not going. This all happened suddenly, so my passport needs to be renewed. Plus I have work and my house. I can't up and go on the spur of the moment."

I wince. Daphne takes a large sip of her wine. She's bouncing her leg under the table. It's her tell that she's stressed. I give her thigh another squeeze, and she gives me a tight smile that doesn't reach her eyes.

"Oh no!" Kendall exclaims. "That's a shame! You can expedite your passport renewal. I'm sure you can get time off and—oof." She gives her brother a dirty look. I'm pretty sure Liam kicked her under the table. There's a reason he's usually my other best friend. When he's not trying to pick up my girl. Thank goodness Kendall is going to school for elementary education and not something like International Relations. She does not have a future in diplomacy.

My mother, bless her soul, starts talking as if the past two minutes didn't happen. "I saw you brought dessert, Daphne. I'm saving room. What is it?"

Dad picks up the conversational baton. "You don't even know what it is, Holly-honey, and you're saving room? What if it's something you don't like?"

Rolling her eyes, she says, "Mike, it's dessert. Of course, I like it."

I love my parents.

Daphne smiles with appreciation at Mom. "It's a caramel apple cake with cream cheese frosting from Half Cocked. I've heard it's delicious. Logan loves their cream cheese frosting from their carrot cake cupcakes."

Aunt Faith chimes in. "It sounds delicious! Thanks so much for bringing it. I love all the apple desserts the season brings. I was thinking it's such a pleasant night we could have dessert out on the patio and light the fire." She gets up from the table. "I know you kids are heading out, but we'll relax out there after you go. Does everyone want coffee with their cake?"

Our fathers trained Liam and me well, so we collect the dishes now that everyone's finished eating. Our dads do the same.

"Do you have any tea, Aunt Faith?" I ask. "Daphne isn't a coffee drinker."

I place mine and Daphne's bowls on the counter while Liam rinses the dishes to prepare them for the dishwasher.

"Oh, no! Don't go to any trouble on my account," Daphne protests.

But Aunt Faith assures her it's not an issue and plugs in the electric kettle she keeps on the counter.

Kendall claps with excitement. "*Ooh!* We have a spicy apple chai and a cinnamon apple rooibos! Which do you prefer?"

"Lipton?" Daphne answers with a sheepish smile.

"Daph isn't fancy about tea," I tell Kennie with a wink.

Mom slices the cake as Aunt Faith prepares a tray for Dad to take to the patio with the coffee mugs, creamer, and sweeteners. The water has heated for the tea, so Daphne's preparing her mug at the breakfast bar. Uncle Will comes in from lighting the outdoor fireplace and takes the tray of cake plates and forks.

"Wow, you folks have dessert service down to a science. I'm impressed!" I say, opening the French doors off the family room to the patio that's more like an outdoor living room.

The deck outside the main bedroom upstairs forms the roof of the space. There's a large table for family dining and a café set for a more intimate meal for two. Conversation seating and a TV make it a fun space to watch baseball on summer evenings. The natural gas-fueled brick fireplace supplies gentle warmth against the chill of the night. This patio is nicer than most people's living rooms.

"Oh my goodness. This space is gorgeous," Daphne says in awe, stepping outside with her mug of tea.

"Yeah, I'd love to have a space like this one day," I say, admiring the area.

"Me too," she replies. "But Gran's house isn't right for a patio this elaborate."

I assume we'll move to something larger when we start a family. But first, we need to figure out what we're doing in order to be together, so I let the matter drop.

We've all chosen to sit on the casual grouping of couches and armchairs rather than the outdoor dining table. I miss times like this —being with my family and Daphne. I've been all around the world, seeing and doing incredible things, but a simple fall evening in New Jersey is exactly where I want to be. I'm fortunate to have these people in my life. Daphne would give anything to spend a carefree Friday night with her parents and Gran, and she never will. I've been taking this for granted.

"Okay, let's go!" Kendall exclaims, practically ripping my cake plate from my hand when I put my last bite in my mouth. "I'm legal now and want to play the slots! This is the first time we've all been out together, and I want to get going."

"I guess that's our cue to leave," I say, standing and pulling Daphne up with me. We say our goodbyes to the parents and get in my Jeep. Kennie and Daphne are in the back, and Liam is riding shotgun.

"We're going to Devil's Den, right?" Kendall asks with her head between the front seats. "The reports on the news when it opened were fantastic. I love how it plays on the Jersey Devil legend. Is Teagan really descended from the family?"

Liam answers. "Yeah, on the maternal side. They're witches. No shifting into the Jersey Devil. I don't think any of them shift. I believe they used spells and misdirection to create the legend."

Now it's Daphne's turn to poke her head between the seats. "You know Teagan Penhall?"

"Yeah, we grew up here and attended college together," Liam confirms. "We're friends."

"Wow, I never knew you traveled in such rarefied circles," she teases.

"Liam's fancy like that," Kennie chimes in as only a younger sibling can.

Instead of playing up the horn-and-tail devil stereotype they could have easily adopted, Devil's Den embraces the old English version of a gambling den. Rich wood finishes, deep-toned leather seating, lighting that's more reminiscent of candlelight than neon. Instead of having the female cocktail servers dressed in a bustier and heels, they wear riding pants, tall boots, and white button-down shirts, like a groom or a gentleman back from his morning ride. There isn't excessive skin showing, but it's sexy. My friend Caleb's sister is a server, and she says the uniforms are extremely comfortable and their tip rates are the highest in the city. The male servers wear the same outfits, and based on the giggles from Daph and Kennie when a server named Simon took our order as we settled at a bank of slot machines, they do wonders for the male employees too.

Kennie stares after the departing server wistfully. "He totally resembles the actor who played Simon! Do you think that's his real name or is it fake to play up on the resemblance? I wish he had the English accent. That would have been perfect. Ooh! Tell him your name is Daphne and see what happens!"

Oh, hell no. I've heard about this Netflix show everyone is gaga over. I'm not letting a Regé-Jean Page doppelgänger near *my* Daphne.

"What the hell, Kendall? You can't be trying to fix up my girlfriend with the cocktail server. Or anyone!" I shake my head. "Where's your loyalty? We're family!"

I'm slightly kidding and being melodramatic, but there's a thread of truth to my statement, too. Just because I'll be leaving in a few days doesn't mean Daphne and I are done. We're in a relationship and exclusive with each other.

Daphne knows that, right?

Oblivious to the thoughts running through my head, Daphne kisses my cheek and settles back to view the animated slot machine in front of her. It's something with lobsters and a bunch of lines to create winning combinations. We're in the penny slot section. It's more about hanging out together and having fun than hardcore gambling.

Studly McStuddington is back with our drinks.

"I got the Coke," I say when he asks.

Liam claims his Guinness beer, and the girls accept their margaritas.

Oh no. They both had wine at dinner, and now they're adding tequila? This is going to be bad. Liam and I make eye contact. He's thinking the same thing I am. He'll watch Kennie and, of course, Daphne is always my focus.

We spend a little time at the slot machines. Kennie's excited. She won twenty bucks on a crazy Yeti-themed game. I'm glad she quit while she's ahead. We wander around the casino floor awash with the noise from the slots and observe the table games. Liam and I play a couple hands of blackjack with no luck, so we don't mind when the girls decide they want to go to the lounge to listen to the live music. One thing that makes Devil's Den unique is that instead of having nightclubs full of thumping bass and sweaty bodies, they have lounges with live music and drink service. It's a bit more refined, and I like it. I enjoy the neon wonderlands of the other casinos, but sometimes it's refreshing to be social in a lower-key atmosphere like this.

The band is very good. They're playing bluegrass-tinged covers of songs made popular by U2, Tom Petty, Africa, and other artists of the last few decades. It's not something you'd expect to work, but it does. There's almost a Celtic tone to it that I appreciate. Somewhere along the way, Kendall and Daphne switch from margaritas to gross candy corn cocktails. My girl's going to be spending her Saturday nursing one hell of a hangover if she doesn't start drinking water and maybe get some good old greasy diner food in her to sop up the liquor.

The girls get up to dance to a rousing version of "Beautiful Day."

Liam leans in and speaks over the music. "We have to cut them off. It's going to be ugly. Did you smell those candy corn monstrosities? They are going to be so much worse coming up than they were going down."

I pick up Daphne's glass, take a sniff, and grimace.

Liam laughs. "How about we wrangle them out of here and hit the diner on the way home?"

The band announces they're taking a break after they finish their song, and now we have a pair of giggling drunk girls back at our table. Pulling Daph in and placing a kiss on her forehead, I murmur, "How about we get out of here, stop at the diner for grub, and then go home? Kennie looks like she's fading fast."

That's a total lie. For a tiny woman, Kendall can drink like a man twice her size. Being a cougar shifter, she can metabolize alcohol quickly. No way can Daphne keep up with her.

Crap, I didn't think about that. Normally Daphne doesn't drink, and we aren't out in a lot of social situations, so it didn't occur to me.

But dangling Kendall's well-being in front of her will fix the situation. Daphne's a nurturer, so if she thinks someone needs taking care of, she's all for it. Under other circumstances, I'd feel guilty misleading her, but it's for her own good.

And I'm right. Daphne's eyes widen, and she flicks a concerned glance toward my cousin. She nods and lets me pull her toward the exit. Kendall and Liam follow close behind.

"I'll wait for the girls. You get the car," Liam says when the girls stop in the restroom on the walk to the valet area. Liam, Kendall, and Daphne appear as the valet returns with my Jeep. Liam's arm hangs around a staggering Daphne, keeping her upright. I know he's being helpful, but he's enjoying his hand around her waist and her body pressed to his side a bit too much for my liking.

I tip the valet and open the passenger side door to help my tipsy girlfriend climb in. I'm not risking her getting carsick in the backseat. I'm suddenly grateful my vehicle is roomy enough that Liam fits in the back without having his knees under his chin.

I don't even make it out of Atlantic City before Daphne is sound asleep, her head resting on the passenger side window as she snores loudly. I guess we're not stopping at the diner.

Kendall leans forward between the seats. "Holy crap. She snores louder than a frat boy!" I meet Liam's wide eyes in the rearview mirror. We silently agree we don't want to know anything about how Kennie knows what frat boys sound like snoring.

Kennie yawns like the cougar she is and falls backward into the seat. "Wanna hit the Mickey D's drive-thru instead of going to the diner? That way, we don't have to get Sleeping Beauty here out of the car and keep her awake long enough to eat."

Kennie is a genius. That is an awesome idea, so I switch lanes to turn into the McDonald's parking lot. I order burgers, fries, and sodas for everyone, along with a hot fudge sundae for Kendall.

"What? I have a fast metabolism," she says defensively.

The scent of greasy, salty goodness rouses Daphne. She sits up and wipes drool off her chin as I pull into a parking spot so we can eat while it's still hot. At least I won't have to juggle fast food bags and my girlfriend into the house if we eat it now.

"Mmpfh, so good," the beautiful woman next to me mumbles, taking a big bite of her double cheeseburger. The slurp of her Diet Coke is the next sound to come from her, causing Liam, Kendall, and me to laugh. Other than her usual Friday night rum and Diet Pepsi to celebrate the end of the work week, Daphne isn't much of a drinker, so for her to imbibe so much tonight is surprising. I'm glad she had fun, but I suspect some of it is because of my upcoming departure. When we all finish our midnight munching, Liam collects our trash and walks it over to the trash can.

"I had fun! Thank you!" Kendall is very perky considering how much liquor she had tonight. I guess it's true that the big cat shifters can process alcohol much faster than other people, even other shifters. She gives me a hug from the backseat and wishes me safe travels. Liam says to text him if I need anything before I go.

After dropping my cousins at their home, I take a shortcut to get to our house so I can tuck Daphne into bed ASAP. Experience tells me this second wind of hers will be brief, and she'll crash again soon. Ideally, I'll have her in our bed before she conks out for good. I guess since Lady Luck wasn't with me at Devil's Den, she favored me by keeping Daph awake and upright long enough to get in the house and ready for bed. Before she settles under the covers, I hand her two aspirin and a bottle of water to wash them down.

Sighing, she snuggles into her pillow. "I had fun tonight, Logan. It's been so long since we've gone out."

She draws her hands under her chin like a child. She is so damn beautiful. My heart hurts. Her lashes kiss her cheeks when she closes her sleepy brown eyes. I lean over and kiss her forehead.

I straighten and am about to leave the room to double-check the locks when I hear her sigh and softly say, "Why are you leaving me? I'm so tired of being left behind. Someday, *someone* is going to stay with me."

Forget hurting. My heart may be breaking. The last thing I want is for Daphne to be sad or feel like she's being abandoned. I need to work. I need to travel to be a travel photographer. That's why it's called that. It's not like there are international kite fairs happening in the backyard or the Portuguese National Horse Fair held at the Atlantic County 4H fairgrounds. I must go where the events are. I don't know how to make her understand this. She would love experiencing these things if she'd give them a chance. I wish she'd go with me, but I don't know how to convince her to stop being so stubborn.

After making sure everything is secure and using the bathroom, I return to the bedroom. Daphne is sleeping peacefully, lying on her side. I strip to my boxers and climb in beside her. Staring up at the ceiling, I watch shadows of the branches of an oak tree outside the window dance on her bedroom wall. I listen to the gentle breathing from the pillow next to me. She's facing away from me since she's most comfortable sleeping on her left side. I didn't know that before this week of sleeping beside her. We've been best friends for years, but there is still so much we don't know about each other. Little things you learn about a person being by their side, day in and day out. I want to know those things about Daph, and I want her to know them about me. I turn on my side and scoot over to spoon her. When I wrap my arm around her and snuggle up against her, she sighs and relaxes against me.

I press a soft kiss to her shoulder and whisper, "I love you."

I wonder, when I finally say it so she can hear me, if she'll say it back.

21

DAPHNE

"Make it stop." I groan at the morning sunlight stabbing its beams into my brain. Why did I drink so much last night? Why did I drink those candy corn cocktails? They were cuter than they were tasty. My mouth feels so gross. Astroturf covers my tongue. Logan must have heard me stirring because he appears in the doorway with aspirin and water.

"Morning, sunshine. Feeling rough?"

He's lucky I know *sunshine* is a term of endearment and not mockery, because sunshine is my mortal enemy at the moment.

I sit up, amazed the room isn't spinning, and take the aspirin from him. I reach for the glass of water and wash down the pills, praying they take effect quickly to ease the pain in my head. Turning the covers aside, I swing my legs out of the bed and sit there, inhaling deep breaths for a few moments before rising. Logan rubs my shoulder gently in a show of comfort.

"I appreciate you want to take care of me, but I feel cruddy, and your touch is annoying the crap out of me," I grouse when I stand up to stumble to the bathroom, locking the door behind me. The Daphne staring back at me from the mirror appears like she's recently crawled out of the swamp. I take care of my morning business and brush my teeth vigorously, swishing an extra helping of mouthwash to eradicate any lingering traces of last night.

"Good plan trying to drink away the pain, Daphne. How did that work for you?" My reflection doesn't answer, so that must mean I'm sobering up. I pray Kendall feels as bad as I do, but I'm betting she doesn't. Lucky duck...um...cougar. I whimper slightly when I run a brush through my hair to tame the oh-so-attractive bedhead I'm sporting. I resemble an electrocuted Muppet, and that's not a good look for me.

I leave the bathroom, and seeing the bedroom is empty, I wander along the hall toward the kitchen. My tea is waiting for me on the counter, and Logan places a plate of toast next to it. The man is a mind reader. I'm not sure my stomach is ready for anything more than tea and toast this morning.

"Thank you. You are the best boyfriend ever. I'm keeping you." I say it in a light tone, but I mean every single word of it.

He sits next to me at the counter with his coffee and bagel with cream cheese and presses a kiss to my temple.

"Try to get rid of me. You're stuck with me. I enjoy taking care of you."

My bite of toast suddenly tastes like sawdust when I think about being alone again after this weekend. I have two more mornings with Logan before he leaves for Spain. I don't know how I'll stand coming home to a quiet house and sleeping alone again. Wow! It's not even been a full week that he's been home, but it feels so...right, like this is how it should always be. I probably shouldn't have drunk so much last night that a hangover ruined the morning. Oh, well. That ship has sailed, so there's nothing to do but make the best of it.

I sip my tea to wash down the toast and look at Logan. He's so handsome in the morning with his hair tousled and stubble dusting his jaw.

"I can't believe you're mine," I say. "I'm so lucky." I lean in to kiss his cheek. His whiskers tickle my lips.

"Was there anything special you wanted to do this weekend? Anything you need to get?" I take another bite of my buttered toast. It's tasting more like bread and less like sawdust, so that's good.

I caught Logan right after he took a bite of his bagel, and he chews and holds up a finger in a *wait a minute* gesture.

Swallowing his bite and then taking a sip of his coffee, he says, "Other than a couple of loads of laundry and repacking my bags, I'm set. We can go out and do whatever you want, or we can hang out here. It's your weekend. I want to do whatever makes you happy." Logan's smile is loving.

My heart hiccups. "I'd love to lock ourselves in this house and spend all of our time cuddling and canoodling until we have to go to the airport."

Logan chortles. "Canoodling?"

I've read the word *chortle,* but I've never seen it in action before. Until now. He has tears from laughing so hard.

"You seriously called what we do together canoodling? Daphne, I've always been very tolerant of your fondness for *Matlock* and *Murder, She Wrote,* but I draw the line at you channeling Jessica Fletcher when you describe our physical relationship."

I'm sure I must be blushing, so I do what any mature woman would do and give him a hard shove in the shoulder to knock him off balance on his stool.

"Canoodling is an awesome word. You're jealous you didn't think to use it first."

His heavy-lidded expression makes my insides quiver. "Sunshine, when I remember the things we've done, canoodling is not the word that comes to mind. When I consider all the things I plan on doing with you, and to you, in the future, it is most definitely nothing that anyone sane and under eighty years old would categorize as *canoodling.*"

Oh my. I'm pretty sure if we were a sitcom, my character would have a thought bubble containing the gif of a cartoon character swooning with hearts in her eyes. But we aren't a sitcom. We're a new couple, having breakfast together, laughing, and trying to ignore the countdown clock until we must part.

Okay, Daphne Marie Foster, stop this train of thought. You're going to ruin the time you have still being together because you're focusing on the time you'll be apart. I know I'm serious because I used my middle name. We have two and a half days together, and I refuse to allow us to waste another moment of that time moping. I'll have weeks to be sad and mopey when he's gone. Why would I waste time that we can spend being together, happy, and creating fun memories being miserable? Of course, it's difficult for Logan to leave, but I don't need to make it even harder by showing him how much I'm dreading it.

I take a sip of my cooling tea. I'm spending too much time thinking and talking and not enough time eating my breakfast. "Have you ever done a corn maze? There are a couple of farms that have them, so we could do one. The Physick Estate in Cape May has a scarecrow walk. Ooh, we could do a ghost tour! I've always wanted to do one of those." I get my laptop so I can start searching for events in Cape May.

Logan grabs his phone. "So...I planned a surprise. If you don't want to do it, it's okay. But what would you say about a weekend in Cape May? I rented a room for tonight. We could sit out on the Adirondack chairs they have set up on the lawn of the hotel. I booked us tickets for a ghost tour, and the hotel is supposed to be haunted. Perfect for this time of year."

I know exactly which hotel he means. It's a grand beachfront hotel. I've always wanted to stay there. "I'd love that! Let me pack a bag."

Logan gasps dramatically.

I jump slightly. "What?"

"You're being spontaneous! I'm so proud of you!" He wipes an imaginary tear from his face.

I huff out a sigh. "I can be spontaneous with little things. Just because I'm not ready to uproot my life on a week's notice doesn't mean I'm not capable of spontaneity." Logan is obviously teasing me, but it hurts a little. "I'm trying, you know."

"Aw...sunshine, I know. I'm teasing. You're wonderful and perfect just the way you are." He leans forward and gives me a sweet kiss, his hand resting on my cheek. His gaze holds so much emotion. Maybe it's love? I hope he sees my love for him as well. Just because I won't allow myself to say it doesn't mean I don't feel it.

"I can't wait to see the pictures you took," I say as we leave the Cape May Zoo. My heartbeat speeds up. "Can I ask a personal question?" It's silly to be so nervous about asking this, and I'm afraid of offending him, but these are things we need to discuss.

Logan glances at me while we wait at the light to get back on the Parkway. "Sure. Twelve inches."

I gape at him and then crack up. "*Not* what I was asking, dude! It's a serious question." He was joking, right? I've felt him, and yeah, he's big, but it didn't seem ginormous. Not that I'm personally familiar with a variety of penises.

"Daph, you can ask me anything. You know that."

The light changes, and I wait for us to make the turn before asking, "Does it bother you, seeing the animals in the cages at the zoos? Especially the eagles?"

We spent a couple of hours walking around, checking out all the animals. My favorites were the giraffes and zebras in the savanna area along the elevated boardwalk. Logan liked the big cats, in particular the snow leopards. There was an enclosure with a bald eagle in it, and it made me sad. I'm aware Logan is a golden eagle shifter, so he's technically different, but the thought of him cooped up upsets me.

"No, why?"

"Well, you're an eagle too. Did you feel a kinship with the bald eagle?"

Logan shoots me a quick glance with a furrowed brow. "Daphne, I'm a man. I shift into an eagle, but I'm human. Those animals there were never human. They've always been animals. For some of them, the sole reason they're alive is because they're in the zoo." He takes my hand and gives it a gentle squeeze. "That zoo isn't an animal jail. They aren't prisoners. They're more like guests. Yeah, there are places where they don't take care of the animals properly or they're made to perform...I hate those things. But I can look at a cougar in a zoo enclosure and separate that from my mom in her shifter form." He checks his mirror and signals to change lanes. "Does it bother you that I'm a shifter?"

I'm shocked he asked me that. "No! There's so much I don't know, so I have questions. I've googled things, but we know that isn't always accurate."

"Okay." He nods. "Of course you'd have questions." We're at the end of the Garden State Parkway, so Logan reduces his speed as we enter Cape May. "You can ask me anything you want. I'll answer you the best I can. Nothing is off limits."

"Anything?"

"Anything."

Okay, here goes. "When you said twelve inches, were you serious? I know shifters are more muscular and stronger, but is that true...everywhere?" I'm not sure it's going to work if that's the case. "It's just a normal penis, right? Nothing weird?"

The car swerves slightly. I don't think he meant I could ask *anything*-anything. He pulls into the parking lot of an elementary school and rests his forehead on the steering wheel, his shoulders shaking with laughter.

He wipes tears from his eyes. If it wasn't about forty miles to walk home, I swear I'd get out of this Jeep and start hoofing it.

"I'm sorry. I don't mean to laugh. It's just...that wasn't a question I expected." He takes a deep breath, turns in his seat, and takes my hand. "Daphne, it's a normal penis. It's not magically going to turn into something crazy like a duck's corkscrew dick or an echidna's four-headed cock when we make love."

I reach for my phone.

"Oh, no! Don't google either of those!" Logan covers my screen with his hand before I can call up Google. "Are you seriously worried about this?"

We've made out and felt each other up, but not a lot below the belt. I wasn't about to have sex for the first time just to be abandoned a week later. Mother Nature helped me out for once by having my period start Tuesday morning, so my resolve didn't get tested.

"Um...you face the possibility of having a twelve-inch thing shoved in you sometime and see how mellow you are about it." I'm trying not to be some kind of cliché virgin scared of a penis, but come on...twelve inches?

"I was joking! No man wants to admit this, but I'm normal-sized." He chuckles. "When the time comes, it will work. Trust me."

Trust him. Because he has experience in this area while I don't. I didn't need that reminder right now.

"Daph..."

Now I have tears. I wipe them away and offer him a smile. We have this weekend together, and I'm not wasting it crying.

"I'm fine," I assure him. "Want to try that hot dog place?"

"Sure," he answers. I can tell he wants to press me on this and discuss it further, but one good thing about being best friends for so long is that he knows when not to push. I'm grateful for that because I want to enjoy the remaining time we have together, not waste it talking about stuff that doesn't matter right now. He's leaving Monday. When he comes home in December, if we're together then, we can talk about it.

I end up with a basic cheese dog, but Logan got creative ordering the Buffalo dog with spicy-hot Buffalo sauce, onions, and bleu cheese.

We sit on a bench on the Promenade, Cape May's concrete version of a boardwalk, and enjoy the view of the ocean. It's cool with the breeze coming off the Atlantic, but the sun is nice, and it's a good excuse to snuggle up against my gorgeous boyfriend. No matter what, he's always warm and toasty. I don't know if it's him naturally, or if it's because he's a shifter, but there are nights in bed it's too much, and I need to shove him away when he wants to snuggle and I don't want to roast.

But at times like this, it's quite handy. Since he finished his hot dog first, he puts his arm around my shoulder while I take the last couple of bites of my dog. He idly toys with the end of my ponytail, wrapping it around his finger and then releasing it. I feel his sigh... and then I smell it.

"Dude! If you're going to be breathing on me after that hot dog, you need to chew gum or pop a breath mint." I crumple up the wrapper from my hot dog and take a sip of my soda before rooting in my bag for the roll of Mentos I keep in there for situations like this.

"Here, take two. You need them." I thumb two out of the roll directly into his mouth. I can feel him laughing as I pop one into my mouth too. My lunch choice was nowhere near as egregious as his, but fresh breath is always pleasant.

Logan glances at his phone to check the time. "We have a couple of hours before our room is ready. How do you want to spend them? We can walk around the shops. Take a trolley tour. Oh, see if they still set the Adirondack chairs up on the lawn, snag a few, and people-watch while enjoying the fresh air." Logan checks to see if any of his ideas spark interest.

They're all appealing, but I'm suddenly struck by something I want to do.

"How about we go play mini golf at Sunset Beach and walk the beach to see if we can find any Cape May diamonds?" I ask. "They have a gift shop too. I have fun poking around in there."

He smirks, and my choice of phrase echoes back to me in a new light.

I groan. "That's the only poking around happening today, buddy. Get your mind out of the gutter."

He laughs as he stands from the bench and holds out his hand to accept the trash from our lunch. "My mind may be in the gutter, but you knew exactly where to find it, sunshine."

I laugh because he's not wrong.

"Mini golf. That sounds fun. I haven't beaten you in mini golf in years."

Scoffing, I rise from the bench. "Dream on, Morris. You have never beaten me at mini golf, and that is not changing today."

It feels like everything else is changing—our relationship, my feelings for Logan, what I want for my life, how I see my life. It's nice to have something remain the same, even if it's something small, like kicking Logan's butt at mini golf.

22

LOGAN

Daphne's right. I'm not beating her at mini golf today. There's a birthday party group playing and a couple of families, so it's crowded. Mini golf is no fun if you feel the need to rush through the course because there's a group waiting to tee off on the hole you're playing.

Daphne bends down and picks up her ball with a nervous glance over her shoulder at the group behind us. She comes to my side and whispers near my ear, her gaze still flicking now and then to the group. "Want to stop playing and check out the gift shop?"

"Sure," I say, grabbing her hand.

We turn in our putters and enter the shop. It's a cute store, having everything from books to food mixes to Christmas ornaments and jewelry. The most important thing right now is the fact that they have sweatshirts. It's windy here at the southern tip of New Jersey, and it's colder than we expected.

"How about we get shirts for now and walk the beach?" Daphne suggests. "I need something more to block the wind."

I nod. "Sounds good. If we want other souvenirs, we can come back in and get them later."

Daphne uses the restroom while I pay for our shirts. Her absence gives me the chance to grab a necklace that caught my attention and add it to my purchase. It's an open heart-shaped silver pendant that appears lacy with a round Cape May diamond in the center suspended from a silver chain. It's not an expensive piece of jewelry, but it's pretty. I can't wait to give my love genuine diamonds and pearls, but I hope she'll like it as a reminder of this day. After paying for everything, I slip the necklace in my pocket and tell the cashier there's no need for a bag for the shirts since we are going to wear them now. I take the receipt and exit the store to wait for Daphne on the porch, ripping the tags off and shoving them in my pocket while waiting. I'm pulling my shirt over my head when I feel my belly being poked. I'm so surprised, I jump and give a bit of a squeal.

"Oh my goodness, you sounded like the Pillsbury Doughboy!" Her uncontrollable laughter sounds like an asthmatic seagull I know. He's a friend of Liam's. She wipes the tears from her cheeks and dries her damp fingers on the thighs of her jeans. I remember one time in college when she was tipsy and started laughing like this. Then she started crying because she laughed so hard, she peed herself a little. Thank goodness she used the restroom already because with how hard she's laughing right now, I'm thinking there could be some sober leakage happening.

I glare at her sternly. "Are you done?" We both know that's an act and I'm one goofy expression away from laughing like a loon myself.

Daph takes a deep breath and composes herself, taking her sweatshirt from my outstretched hand.

With a direct gaze, she answers, "No, not at all."

Sighing, I thread her fingers with my own and tug her toward the beach. The wind carries her giggles away.

Even though it's windy and cold, it's nice to walk along Sunset Beach with Daphne, searching for Cape May diamonds. We decide not to collect any of the quartz stones, but Daph finds a pretty green piece of sea glass that we can't leave behind. I've been to beautiful beaches all around the world with crystal blue water, white sand, black sand, roiling waves, calm seas—you name it, I've seen it. But I think this beach on the Delaware Bay at the southern tip of New Jersey is my favorite beach ever.

"Daph?"

"Yeah?"

"Are we okay?"

She gazes up at me quizzically. "Yeah. Aren't we?"

I can't articulate what I mean. My instinct is to leave it at that and lean in for a quick kiss. However, that won't progress our relationship.

"I leave Monday."

"I'm well aware of that, Logan."

I let out a huff of frustration. Why isn't she making this easy for me?

"I feel like there's a lot we need to talk about before I go," I say.

"There is," she agrees, "but I don't want to talk about it now."

"Daph, come on..."

"Not now." There's an edge to her voice she usually doesn't use when speaking to me.

"When?"

"Later." She sighs, her shoulders slumping. "I just want to enjoy today. Enjoy being together while we still can." Daphne shivers. "I'm becoming a popsicle. How about we drive back to town and check into our room? I saw a coffee shop, and if they're still open, I want hot cocoa."

I drop her hand and wrap my arms around her. She hugs me in return, slipping her fingers under both my sweatshirt and long-sleeved T-shirt to put her icy hands against my bare back. I let out a manly yelp because it's like being caressed by an ice cube tray, and Daphne laughs. She's loving torturing me today. That's okay, I have my own ways of getting revenge.

"Yeah, I'm ready," I say. "I wasn't expecting it to be so much cooler here. I guess I should have. It's late October, but it's been mild.

The air off the water makes a difference." We disengage from our hug, and I take her hand again.

I give her chilled digits a gentle squeeze.

"Let's warm you up. Can't have my sunshine be cold."

"Logan?" Daphne's taking her turn with twenty questions, apparently. "I love that you call me sunshine. When I was little, my dad would sing 'You Are My Sunshine' to me when he'd tuck me in. Mom recorded it on video. I wish I had it. Our basement flooded, and it ruined our VHS videos." Her eyes mist over. "That was when I was thirteen, so I obviously wasn't being tucked in anymore. I didn't realize I'd never get to hear him sing that to me again." She takes a deep breath.

I reach out to brush away the tear slipping down her cheek. "I wish I had known your parents. I wish you still had them. It breaks my heart how much it hurts you to have lost them." I can't imagine the loss she's suffered. I've never lost someone close to me. Even all my grandparents are still living.

Shrugging, Daphne gives a small smile. "They would've loved you. Well, Mom would have. She would've thought you were charming. Dad probably would've suspected you and your intentions toward his little girl."

I wiggle my brows to lighten the mood and because we both know I have all sorts of intentions involving Daphne. Most of them are honorable and pure, but there are a few that are a bit lascivious.

It works.

She giggles and bumps her shoulder against my arm as we return to my Jeep.

"Ultimately he'd have liked you because you make me happy and you care about me. I imagine that's what they would want for me."

We fall into silence on our drive to Cape May. I hope the Fosters would have approved of me. All I want is to make Daphne happy and love her for the rest of our lives. I need to figure out how to make that happen and get her to open up to me. As much as I want her body—

and wow, do I desire her body—I can't wait for us to take our relationship to the next level.

However, what I truly want is her heart and for her to trust me
enough to share the thoughts and fears in her beautiful head. She's
keeping stuff from me, and frankly, it hurts. We're best friends.
Forget that we're exploring a romantic relationship. We've known
each other for years. We should trust each other with our truths and
especially our fears, not hide from each other. I don't want to ruin
our weekend by pushing her too hard, but I don't want to leave
Monday with everything unsaid.

———————

"Oh wow, this view is magnificent!" Daph is at the window, sipping
her cocoa and enjoying the view out over the grand lawn and the
Atlantic Ocean. "What time is sunrise? A bit after seven in the morning, right? If we're awake, we'll be able to watch it."

I wasn't able to get a room with a balcony, but the four-poster
bed faces a double window that has a window seat decorated with
pale blue cushions, so we could watch the sunrise from bed, snuggling under the white duvet, or while cuddling on the window seat.
The king-size bed is dark wood, but the desk, dresser, and nightstands are painted bright white. The white of most of the furnishings
and bedding paired with the pale blue walls and blue striped
carpeting gives the room a bit of a beach cottage feel. I guess that's
appropriate since the Atlantic Ocean is right outside our window.

"Oh my goodness," Daphne calls out. "This bathroom is
gorgeous, and the lotion smells so nice."

I hope to rub it all over her tonight. I bet they sell it downstairs.
I'll have to get a supply for home if it feels as good as it smells.

"Where do you want to go for dinner?" I ask. "There are a lot of
great restaurants in Cape May, so you can't make a wrong choice."

Exiting the bathroom, Daph replies, "The Ghosts of Cape May
trolley tour is a quarter after seven, so we should do something on

the Mall." She quirks her lips to the side, the classic Daphne Foster thinking face. She names a restaurant we've enjoyed before.

"Perfect. I could go for a burger and a beer."

Not wanting to seem like tourists, we change out of the Cape May hoodies that we bought at the Sunset Beach Gift Shop. I exchange my navy hoodie for a dark green V-neck sweater over my gray long-sleeve T-shirt, and Daphne swaps her light blue sweatshirt and T-shirt for a thin black turtleneck sweater that lovingly caresses her curves and one of my red plaid flannel shirts. What is it with her stealing my shirts? I admit, it's much cuter on her than it is on me. She's rolled up the sleeves since her arms aren't as long as mine. With her blue jeans and black Converse sneakers, she's casual but put together. I pull out my phone to take a picture of her to remember this moment.

Daph spins around to put her back to me. "What are you doing? Stop!" She hates having her picture taken. I'm amazed she agreed to do the selfies at the lighthouses.

"Sunshine, turn around. I don't have nearly enough pictures of you. I've taken thousands, more likely hundreds of thousands, of pictures of people and places all around the world, but I only have a few of you." That's crazy. She's the most beautiful sight in the world to me, and I haven't captured her visage nearly enough. I could take her picture for hours every day and not do justice to how lovely she is. But I want to try. "Please?" She heaves an enormous sigh and turns back around. The pink on her cheeks is adorable. I know posing makes her feel awkward, so I hit a few buttons on my phone, walk over, and kiss her like my life depends on it. I hear the click as the phone takes a series of pictures, and I'm sure that the last shot of the two of us, with our foreheads pressed together and soft smiles on our lips, will be my favorite.

As we look through the shots, she asks, "Are you happy now?"

I love how Daphne's head is resting back against my chest as I hold my phone in front of us to scroll through the pictures. I want to stay like this forever.

I kiss the crown of her head. "I will be once you talk to me. Can we discuss things when we come back here after our tour?"

I wrap my arm a bit more securely around her waist before she can bolt. I can feel her tense, so I loosen my hold a touch. I don't want her to feel restrained. I'm relieved she doesn't pull away.

"Yeah," she sighs. "When we get back."

Stepping away from me, she gives me the fake cheery smile she uses to hide from the world. I hate it. She doesn't know I've figured out what that smile means, so I ignore it for now. We can't keep ignoring everything and putting it off until later. We need to deal with things. But first we'll have dinner and go on a tour.

23
DAPHNE

I PEER OVER MY MENU AT LOGAN. HE'S SO HANDSOME IN HIS DARK GREEN sweater. I love how it deepens the Christmas tree green of his eyes. He'll be home for Christmas this year, so maybe we can decorate a tree together. I haven't done a tree the past couple of years because it's just me, but if it will be the two of us, I'd like to do something. I have the decorations from my family growing up and Gran's too. There's a Christmas shop here on the Mall. Maybe we can find an ornament to remember this time. Or not. Maybe it's stupid to plan for something that's probably not going to happen. He's going to go to Europe and will get involved in stuff and not come home for Christmas. He does this every year. But he's never broken a promise to me. He hasn't said he'd come home and then didn't. He just doesn't commit.

I refocus on the menu to avoid the rising sadness. "I'm getting a grilled ham and cheese. Want to split a basket of fries?"

Logan smiles. "Yeah, fries sound good. I'm getting the bacon cheeseburger. I'll eat your pickle."

I can't help it. I snort-laugh because that sounded kinky, and there are times I have the sense of humor of a twelve-year-old boy.

He smirks, which tells me he's about to make a suggestive comment back, but our server's arrival stops him.

"Hi, I'm Steve. Can I get you something from the bar or an appetizer to start?" Steve is around our age, with dark blonde hair flopping in his bright blue eyes. He's handsome.

I smile up at him. "Hi, Steve. I think we're ready to order everything. I'd like an unsweetened iced tea and the grilled ham and cheese on rye. Can I get that with Swiss cheese, please?"

"For you, beautiful, absolutely." Steve winks.

I feel myself flush. I'm not used to this kind of attention. He turns to Logan and asks what he'd like.

Logan orders his bacon cheeseburger, a basket of fries to share, and a Guinness.

After Steve walks away to place our order with the kitchen and get our drinks, I ask, "What's up with ordering fries to quote, *share with my girlfriend*, end quote?" I even do air quotes to be extra obnoxious. Why should Logan have a monopoly on the trait?

"He was flirting with you. That's not cool."

What the hell? Logan's never jealous.

I reach out and grab his hand where it rests on the table and lace our fingers together. "Who cares? I'm here with you, and there's no one else I want to be with. You didn't have to metaphorically pee on me to stake your claim."

He unlaces our fingers but lifts my hand to his lips to press a kiss to my palm. "I'm going to sound like an asshole saying you're mine, but you are. I don't like other guys trying to pick you up. You don't recognize it, but guys flirt with you all the time."

I scoff. "No, they don't! Guys never notice me."

Steve comes up to the table with our drinks. "Guys totally notice you. I was flirting with you." He gestures with his chin. "Those two guys at the bar are checking you out. Your boyfriend is the luckiest man in here tonight."

I'm flabbergasted, but curious. "I'm obviously here with someone. Why bother flirting with me?"

Steve shrugs. "There's always the chance he's your brother, or the date doesn't turn out well. I want to save my place in line. It's a pretty successful strategy."

I blink. I'm pretty sure that's the skeeviest thing I've ever heard. "Oh."

Steve walks away, and Logan flashes me an *I told you so* expression. He's so annoying when he's right.

"Are girls more attractive when they're with a guy? No one usually pays attention to me."

Logan looks at me like I'm daft. "Daphne, guys have always paid attention to you. You just don't recognize it."

I don't believe him. "Name one," I challenge him.

"Soccer Matt, Ben, Ferd, Baseball Matt, Liam. Shall I go on?" Logan leans back in the booth with his arms across his chest and a smirk on his face. He named four guys we knew in college off the top of his head. They were classmates of ours, and a couple were friends of his. Ferd was his roommate. His cousin, Liam? No way.

"None of those guys in college ever asked me out. They were not interested in me."

I see red creep up Logan's neck. "Well, I made it known you were off limits."

What the ever-loving hell? My hands ball into fists on the table, and my jaw tightens so hard I think it might break. Thank goodness I don't have any mystical powers because there would be lasers shooting through my eyes as well.

He knows he's in trouble because the words spill out all at once as he rushes to explain. "None of them were good enough for you. They were all hit-it-and-quit-it types. You deserved someone who would date you and appreciate you. Obviously, if I could discourage them so easily, they weren't worthy of you. You deserve to be fought for." His eyebrows furrow. "None of the college guys asked you out. What about Liam? Has he asked you out?"

"Not seriously, and anyway, I've never said yes." I don't know why I'm reassuring him. He's not off my shit list yet. I didn't want to date any of those guys. They were each cute in their own way, but none of them gave me butterflies the way Logan always has. But it was for *me* to decide. It wasn't Logan's place to stop anything before it even started. If he knew what I deserved, then why didn't he step up and be that man sooner?

His ability to read my mind is on point tonight because he responds as if I asked the question aloud.

"I was an idiot. I knew those guys weren't worthy of you. I had opinions on what you deserved, and I didn't think I fit the bill either. I wanted to sow a few wild oats, and I valued our friendship. I didn't see how I could have it all—friendship, adventure, a physical relationship—with you."

I flinch. Hearing that hurts.

Logan reaches out for my hand again, remorse in his expression. "Chalk it up to being young and dumb, not recognizing you were everything I wanted and needed. Obviously, we still need to figure out details, but I know, together, we can have everything I've always wanted. We can have it all."

I smile, but it feels tight, and I pull my hand away from his, wrapping it around the cool tumbler of iced tea. The icy glass cools my anger and my hand.

I stare at Logan and say with an atypical directness for me, "You were an idiot, but so was I. There's no reason I couldn't have told you how I felt or approached guys if I was interested in them." I stretch out my leg under the table to tap his foot with mine. "We are in the twenty-first century, not a Jane Austen novel. I can go for what I want. I don't have to wait for a man to decide I'm worthy of his attention."

I take another sip of my iced tea. If I'd known we were having this type of dinner conversation, I would have opted for the Long Island version. "I accept I was passive in our relationship when I could have approached you to see if you were interested in more, but I was afraid you wouldn't and then I'd lose your friendship. Or, even worse, what if we tried, and it didn't work out? I would have lost your friendship, had my heart broken, and been all alone. I'm not sure I was strong enough then to handle that."

I grab his Guinness and take a sip because I need something stronger than iced tea. Placing the glass back on the table in front of him, I swallow and lick any foam that may be along my top lip. His gaze follows my tongue when it sweeps across my lip. I do it again to mess with him, causing him to take a sip as well, turning the glass so his lips land where mine recently were. Wow, that's kind of hot.

"Here we go! Bacon cheeseburger." Steve, the mood killer, places Logan's burger on the table. "Grilled ham and Swiss on rye for the beautiful lady." He winks at me as he lowers my plate in front of me. "And a basket of fries for the lovebirds to share." With his tray now empty, he puts it under his arm and asks if there's anything else we need. We order refills of our drinks. I'm sticking with my nonalcoholic choice. We can always have a nightcap back at the hotel.

Logan adds ketchup to his burger and grabs the pickle off my plate. I can't stand pickles, so it's nice to have a dining companion that will get rid of mine for me. I take a bite of my sandwich and barely suppress a groan. It's so good.

Both of us have our mouths full when Steve brings our drinks, so we nod our thanks.

Swallowing his bite of burger, Logan conversationally says, "You know, we could always skip the tour and go back to the hotel."

It's a tempting idea because our remaining time together is limited, but I want to do more than make out with my boyfriend, Logan, all the time. I want to spend time with my *friend* Logan too. I know what to expect from friend Logan. He can't disappoint me. Boyfriend Logan could break my heart, and I'm not sure it can survive another blow.

I shake my head. "We already bought our tickets taking spots someone else could have had, and I want to do the tour. I want to see how they do it. When we'd take tours when I was younger, I'd drive my parents crazy, asking them what their favorite parts were and taking notes on how I'd do it better. I used to write out scripts for tours I'd want to do. One video that got ruined when the basement flooded was me dressed as a tour guide for Halloween and giving a tour of the neighborhood as I trick-or-treated. I was pointing out trees that still had leaves, mentioning which houses put up the best holiday decorations, who had friendly dogs, silly stuff like that."

"You know our hotel is haunted, right?" Logan smiles. "Maybe we'll see one tonight."

I'm working my way through the basket of fries now that I've finished my sandwich, and I wave my fry as I answer. "I knew that! Rumor is this restaurant is haunted too. There are quite a few ghosts here on the Washington Street Mall. I have a couple of books about Cape May hauntings. Did you know *Ghost Hunters* did an episode at the Southern Mansion? Maybe we can stay there the next time we visit."

"Would you want to give ghost tours?" Logan asks. "I love ghost stories for the historic insights they give. It's a way for the average person to be known when they didn't live a life deemed exciting enough for a history textbook."

I shake my head. "Nah, I'm afraid I'd bring my work home with me."

His bark of laughter makes me grin. Steve arrives to clear our plates and ask if we'd like anything else, leaving our check when we assure him we're done. Logan puts cash to cover the check and Steve's tip in the bill holder, and with a smirk, shows me the check. Steve wrote *You're a lucky man, dude. Have a great night.* Standing, Logan puts out a hand to help me rise from the booth.

Holding hands, we exit the restaurant, waving to Steve as we leave.

"We have about half an hour before the tour. Want to window shop on our way to the loading spot?" Logan is swinging our arms while we walk. It's so carefree, and I love it.

"Yeah, sounds good," I reply. "We have to get fudge, so we need to pop in there on the way back to the room."

We stretch the five-minute walk to the trolley pick-up point with window shopping. We decide that after the tour, we'll check out the selection of mystery jigsaw puzzles in the toy shop. Logan's parents enjoy assembling jigsaw puzzles together and reading mysteries. Combining them in one activity sounds like a great possible Christmas gift.

The trolley is allowing passengers on when we arrive. We climb aboard and take seats toward the back. The tour guide is very knowledgeable and shares a few spooky tales of hauntings throughout town. I wish the tour was longer. I loved the experience of riding on the trolley through the streets of this beautiful historic town, listening to stories and being snuggled next to Logan. If he comes home, maybe we'll come back and take more tours. There are several of them closer to Christmas. Or maybe I'll just take them by myself. Or not.

On our visit to the toy shop, we decide on a Titanic murder mystery jigsaw puzzle for his parents for Christmas. At his suggestion, I cross the Mall to the fudge shop while he waits in line to pay.

"I want chocolate chip and chocolate peanut butter. How about you?" I ask Logan when he joins me, perusing the variety of fudge behind the glass.

"I like plain vanilla. What about Snickers?"

We end up with two pounds of fudge in a variety of flavors. It freezes, so there may be some left when Logan comes home. Or maybe not if I eat my feelings. We get a free box of saltwater taffy, too. There will be some of that for Logan, since I don't like all the flavors.

Wandering back to the hotel hand in hand, we admire the beautiful houses we pass. Many are bed and breakfasts, but a few are private homes. I can't imagine what it would be like to live in one of these houses and raise a family. It's such a vacation destination. It must be weird to be here when the town is quiet.

"I love these Victorians," I say. "I wonder what it's like to live in one."

He considers it. "They are beautiful, but they're so jammed

together, and you have to deal with the summer traffic. I'd rather live in one closer to home. There are beautiful ones along Shore Road that would be stunning with a bit of work. They have yards too. If your heart isn't set on a Victorian, there are colonial homes in Port, not that they come up for sale often, but we have time. We can be patient."

I cock my head to the side. "Why would we be house hunting? We have a house." We've reached the hotel and are climbing the stairs to our room. Logan lets go of my hand to remove our room key from his front pocket and unlocks the door. I walk in ahead of him and turn on a few lights.

"It's not that big of a house. We'll outgrow it when we have kids." Logan peers at me like this should be obvious.

When did kids enter the picture? He leaves the day after tomorrow, and we haven't done any baby-making activities yet, so there's no possibility of kids anytime soon.

"You want kids, don't you?" The uncertainty on Logan's face and in his voice isn't something I'm used to.

Shrugging, I reply, "I've never really thought about it."

"Really?" He sounds surprised.

"Really. Why plan for a future that probably won't happen? You know the saying—make plans and God laughs. I've learned that lesson well. If I ever get married, I'll think about it then."

"If you ever get married?" He's pacing in front of the windows. "What do you think we're doing?"

Is this a trick question? "We've been together for a week, and you leave the day after tomorrow for a month and a half. We aren't getting married. We're barely dating."

A flash of hurt crosses his face. What is that about?

"I assumed this was a temporary thing while you were here," I say. "When you came home, we'd see where we were and maybe do it again?"

Right? We're going to be apart, so how would we keep this going?

"Are you putting a time limit on our relationship?" I'm not used to hearing anger in Logan's voice. Especially directed at me.

"What? No! I'm just trying to be realistic. You're gone ten months out of the year, Logan! How am I supposed to make that work?"

"Daphne, why is it realistic to think we'll not be together forever?"

His question brings me up short. "Nothing lasts forever. My parents didn't last forever."

"Oh, Daph." Logan reaches out and pushes a strand of hair behind my ear and caresses my cheek. Closing my eyes, I press my cheek against his palm, savoring the warmth and wanting to imprint it on my brain to remember when he's gone. "They're the textbook definition of forever. They died together. Didn't live a day apart since they wed."

I blink back the hot tears that have suddenly gathered in my eyes and pull away. "Okay, nothing lasts forever *for me*. I don't get forever. Everyone leaves me, and I get left behind."

"You know that's not true, Daphne. Your parents died in a tragic accident. They didn't choose to leave you. Your grandmother was old and sick. It wasn't her choice." Logan tries to embrace me.

I give a harsh laugh and pull away from him. "So, it's only you that chooses to leave me? You talk about forever, but all you ever do is leave."

"I'm not *leaving* you. I'm going to work. I always come back to you. And you aren't left behind. You choose not to go! I've asked you countless times to join me, and you always say no."

"I have to work too! I need the health insurance my job provides. I need to pay taxes on the house and pay my bills. My savings would only cover me for six months."

"So come with me for six months! We'll figure it out."

I sit on the bed, exhausted. Today was like a dream come true, and now it's turned into a nightmare.

Logan sits next to me on the bed. I rest my head on his shoulder, and he wraps his arm around me. I don't want to waste our time together fighting. I want to enjoy this time and have memories to cherish all the days I'm alone.

"I'm always going to come back to you, Daphne," Logan repeats.

He believes that, but my parents expected to come back home that night too. Every time he leaves, there's a chance he's not coming home to me. It doesn't matter if he chooses to leave me or if something takes him from me, I'll be alone again.

I don't want to fight anymore. I want to go to bed, to feel his arms around me and ignore the fact that in less than forty-eight hours, I'll say goodbye to him.

"Okay," I say to end this. "Can you hold me, please?" I raise my head to place a kiss on his jaw.

"I want nothing more, sunshine," Logan says, placing a gentle kiss on my temple. We help each other undress and hold each other under the covers. Even after everything we've said tonight, there's so much left unsaid between us. The ghosts aren't the only things haunting this room tonight. Logan falls asleep first, and I let the rhythmic sound of his breathing and the soothing beat of his heart under my head pillowed on his chest lull me to sleep.

24
LOGAN

I'm rarely a big fan of Monday mornings, but this one inspires a special kind of loathing. I leave today, and I dread going. I'm in our bedroom, putting the last of my clothes in my bag.

"Are you sure you don't want me to ask Liam to take me to the airport or hire a car?"

I need to be at the international airport in Philly in four hours for my late afternoon flight to Madrid. I'll arrive in Spain early tomorrow morning. I regret not adjusting my schedule so that I had more time here with Daphne. I didn't expect it to be so hard to leave her. Truth be told, I didn't expect to be leaving her behind. I thought she would join me. I should've known she wouldn't drop everything and run away with me. Usually, I appreciate her steadiness, but now it's just something else keeping us apart.

"Hush. I want to spend every moment possible with you before you leave. I'm taking you to the airport. That's why I took today off," she scolds me.

We woke in each other's arms Sunday morning and ignored our heated words from the night before. We need to talk about our future, and I need to know that we're on the same page, but I don't want to ruin the little time we have left by upsetting Daphne again. I didn't realize how deeply the deaths of her parents and grandmother had affected her. I knew she was sad, and I knew she missed them, of course, but I didn't realize how abandoned she felt.

I don't know how to reassure her. I can't stay. I need to work. If she wanted to be together, she could come with me.

"Is that the mail truck?" I ask, trying to get Daphne out of the bedroom. Wow, never thought I'd think that thought.

"I'll go check," she says, starting down the hallway. I put the necklace I purchased at the gift shop at Sunset Beach under Daph's pillow. I daydream about her finding it there at bedtime. I've left a few of my shirts behind, unsaid messages that I'm coming back, that even when I'm gone, I want her wrapped up in me. The shirts mark her as mine when she thinks there is no us. Especially then.

I snagged the tank top she wore to bed last night. I'm not going to wear it. A man wearing a woman's shirt is nowhere near as sexy as a woman wearing a man's shirt. Plus, my abs are too ripped to pull off the Winnie-the-Pooh style effectively. I'd need more of a belly to give the proper vibe. Anyway, the shirt is for cuddling purposes. I also packed a little bottle full of Daphne's shampoo, so I can sniff it when I'm missing her. That's not weird. Okay, it *is* weird, but it won't get me strange attention from the TSA agents like a pair of her panties would. Of course, I'm sure they've seen it all. Panties in my luggage probably wouldn't earn me any raised eyebrows.

I come up behind Daphne where she's standing at the counter going through the mail, wrap my arms around her waist, and rest my chin on her shoulder, nuzzling behind her ear and chuckling when she shivers. That's one spot I can always elicit a response from with proper attention.

"Anything interesting?" I ask, seeing the mail pile.

"You got an envelope, but other than that, it's junk," she replies, passing me an envelope over her shoulder. I don't recognize the New York City return address, so it can't be anything too important. I put it on the counter and resume nuzzling Daphne.

"Aren't you going to open it?" she asks. She turns in my embrace so we're facing each other.

I press a soft kiss to her lips. All I want to do is spend our remaining time together kissing and holding her, but we must show restraint. I don't need to be going through security with a prominent hard-on. If we continue this way, that will be the situation.

I pull back from our kiss. "I'll open it later. I'm sure it's nothing important." My stomach growls. "What do you want to do for lunch? We can stop somewhere to eat on the way to the airport, or we can make sandwiches and hang out here a bit longer."

Our best plan is to head out because the longer we stay here, the more difficult it will be for me to leave when it's time. This little house has become my home this past week. Yeah, I've lived here before, but it's been the place I stayed between jobs. It's not been my home until now.

My home is wherever Daphne is.

Daphne presses her lips together. "We've got leftovers, but"—she heaves a tremendous sigh and looks away from me—"let's just go." She must know what I do—we can't start saying goodbye until we leave, and the longer we stay, the harder it will be.

"Let's eat on the way. If we stay here, there's a chance I'll seduce you and tie you to the bed," she jokes.

It's on the tip of the tongue to tell her if she seduces me, I'd stay forever, but I don't want her to think I'm leaving because we haven't had sex yet. I'm not an asshole like that. Instead, I laugh, knowing she's messing around.

"Honey, I'm up—literally and figuratively—for tying each other to the bed, and I'm willing to be the first one tied up because I'm a giver like that."

Okay, Logan, stop thinking about bondage because it's going to be a hellacious flight if you can't lower the tray table because your cock is hard and in the way.

While Daphne dresses, I double-check my bags to ensure I have my passport and other documents in order. I snag the envelope that came in today's mail and slip it in the pocket of my carry-on. I'll read it eventually. I need to check a bag for my clothing and camera accessories like tripods, flashes, and lenses, but the important things like my camera bodies, the most expensive lenses, a flash, memory cards, and my laptop go in my carry-on bags. I don't let them out of my sight. It's much easier to buy new underwear than replace thousands of dollars worth of gear. Everything is in order like I expected it to be. I've packed my belongings so often it's more or less muscle memory at this point.

Gorgeous in her jeans and purple sweater, Daph emerges from our bedroom. "Ready to go?"

No, I'm not.

"Yeah, I have everything. Let's go," I say instead as I grab my bags, glancing around the living room at the couch where we've spent the past week cuddling, and follow Daphne out the front door, making sure the lock has engaged. The next time I come home, the pots of brightly colored mums we bought for the porch will be dead and gone. I miss them already.

I'm missing pots of flowers. It's ridiculous. I've seen the tulip fields of the Netherlands, visited beautiful gardens of grand homes, explored tropical rain forests, and I'm lamenting pots of chrysanthemums.

Climbing in the driver's seat of Daphne's Escape after putting my bags in the back, I ask about lunch. "Want to stop for burgers at the place on 42?"

There's a 1950s-themed restaurant on a road we can take to the airport. Most of the time we'd take the Atlantic City Expressway since it's faster, but I'm not in a hurry to get to the airport, and this way we can stop for lunch.

"Sure, sounds good. I haven't been there in forever." My girl puts a brave smile on her face. "It's a shame we won't have time for the arcade. I guess that means we'll have to go back."

She's doing her absolute best to be cheery and make it easy for me to leave. She knows if I know she's upset, it will gut me. However, the forced cheeriness is twisting a knife in my stomach all the same. Leaving has never been this difficult before. I always miss Daphne when I go, but my eagerness to be off on my next adventure usually tips the scales in favor of leaving. That's not the case this time. For the first time, I feel apathetic over my departure, and if I was being honest with myself, I'd admit what I'm really feeling is dread.

We pull into the restaurant parking lot. It's been years since we've eaten here, and I hope it's as good as I remember. Well, years since *I've* eaten here. For all I know, Daphne comes here all the time. Without me.

I recognize the hypocrisy of moping over things Daphne has done in our places without me while I've been off traveling the world. It doesn't help ease the ache though.

"It doesn't seem like anything has changed," I say, holding the door for her. This place is cool. It resembles an old 1950s diner like from *Happy Days*, with mini jukeboxes at each booth. The female servers wear pedal pushers or poodle skirts, and the male servers wear cuffed jeans and white T-shirts, channeling The Fonz. The burgers and fries are incredible, and they have a soda fountain where you can order all kinds of exotically flavored sodas, ice cream floats, and milkshakes. There's an arcade attached full of video games and boardwalk games like Skee-Ball. Sometimes in college, we'd come with rolls of quarters and spend the entire afternoon playing games and goofing off, giving our stash of tickets to a kid so they could cash them in for prizes. Those were wonderful days.

"Hey, hon, you can sit wherever you want. I'll bring over menus," the waitress calls out to Daphne as we enter.

"Thanks," Daph responds. "Booth by the window?"

Nodding, I follow her to the booth, unable to resist resting my hand on Daph's lower back as we walk over. I don't want to pass up any opportunity to touch her. She must feel the same way because instead of sitting across from each other like we usually do, she grabs my hand and pulls me to sit beside her. I wrap my arm around her shoulders as our waitress comes over with menus and two glasses of water.

"She waited on us last time, didn't she?" It is obvious Daphne is on the same wavelength as I am.

"I think so. I remember the eyeglasses." I read over the menu even though I already know what I'm getting. "What sounds good to you?"

"Other than you?" With a cheeky grin, Daphne leans in to kiss me. "I'm thinking about the double cheeseburger. Want to split an order of cheese fries?"

That sounds good. I nod my agreement when our waitress, Marcia, approaches our table.

"Ready to order?" Marcia asks, pad in hand.

"I love your glasses!" Daphne enthuses, smiling up at her.

"Thanks, hon!" They are cute, pink cat-eye shaped with rhinestones in the corner. Very kitschy, but it fits the vibe of the place.

"I'll go first." Daphne places her order. After I give my order and Marcia walks away, Daph taps our menus on the table and puts them back in the holder.

Stretching my arm along the back of the booth, Daphne snuggles into my side, placing her hand on my thigh. I press a kiss to her temple and sigh. We haven't spoken much since we got in the car, and there's so much to say. I think we're afraid of getting emotional and making our parting even more difficult, so we're choosing to remain silent instead. I'm fearful that if I express any reluctance or doubt about leaving, Daphne will ask me to stay, and I'll be in the position of having to tell her no.

Not that she has any problem telling me no when I ask her to come with me. Okay, that sounded bitter. I understand why she says no. I don't like it, but I understand it. I'm not wasting our limited time together on bitterness. That's what my flight to Madrid is for.

Technically, I could cancel this trip and stay here. I'm a freelancer, and I'm not under contract with anyone. However, I know the events I'm attending create the shots that sell well. My plan is to shop my photos around to some publications and websites I've worked with before and also use some images to bolster my stock photo catalog.

I need to spend my downtime on this trip to investigate more of the business side of things and how I can create a passive income with shots I've already taken, so I'm able to adjust my travel schedule. I can't travel ten months of the year and maintain a relationship. If I show I'm willing to sacrifice, then maybe Daphne will be comfortable joining me. She's right. I blindsided her, showing up out of nowhere and asking her to drop everything and run away with me. My life would be easier if she had. But I hadn't realized then how deep her issues go.

"It will be okay, Logan." Daphne squeezes my thigh. "We're best friends. I know you. You must go because you have things planned. It's okay. But we need to figure things out. If we're dating, I don't want to spend long stretches of time apart beyond this."

I'm aware she doesn't have paranormal gifts, but, in this moment, I swear she's a mind reader.

She sighs. "We both need to compromise. I need to figure out how to do that. It's difficult for me."

I take a deep breath. "I'm aware we have a lot to work out but didn't address this week. We'll spend the next weeks figuring out a game plan that works for both of us. It'll be okay." That last part is more to reassure me than her.

"Here we go!" Marcia announces, placing our burgers and a basket of fries before us. "Ketchup and napkins are there." She juts her chin toward the caddy near the window. "Do you need anything else at the moment?"

"We're good," I say, smiling at her.

Daphne hands me the ketchup and a few extra napkins so I can doctor my burger. There's that happy groan again when Daph takes her first bite of burger. I need to get a recording of it so I can make it a ringtone on my phone. Or play it on a continuous loop while I imagine how wonderful it will be to finally be with Daphne completely, body and soul.

Lunch was delicious, as expected, and much sooner than I'd like, we're back in the car, headed to the airport. It's crazy how one week has changed my life and my plans for it. I don't know what I expected. That I'd come home, make her mine, and then take off again without it breaking my heart if I had to leave her behind?

God, I'm an idiot.

"I think this is the fastest I've gotten to this airport," I say, pulling up in front of the terminal for my airline. The traffic gods can suck it.

Putting the car in park and turning off the engine, I turn to Daphne. She's so beautiful with the loving smile she gives as she reaches for her door handle. I'm tempted to hit the lock so we remain trapped in here and I can't leave. But I don't. I check for traffic and then exit to meet Daphne at the back with the open hatch.

I take her in my arms. "Daph, this is going to be hard, and I know we're going to miss each other. You're worried about me. I'm worried about you. This is going to suck. But it's six weeks. It's not forever."

I'm saying this just as much, if not more, for me as I am for her. It's not working. Six weeks feels like forever.

She takes a deep breath, but she's not fooling me. She's putting on a brave face to make this easier on me.

"You're going to these amazing places and will take incredible pictures, pictures so wonderful there are going to be people clamoring to buy them and license them. You're going to tell me all about what you see and experience when we FaceTime like we always do. It's going to be okay."

Her arms wrap around my torso, and she buries her head against my chest as my arms encircle her. I don't want to let go, but after a few moments, I do. This will be okay. Releasing Daphne and stepping back, I tuck a strand of her dark brown hair behind her ear and caress her cheek.

"Sunshine, you are incredible. I'm so lucky you're my girl."

Resting her palm on my cheek, she smiles. "You are so lucky, but so am I. Now you're going to have to go check in and get through security before they bug us to move the car. I don't want our goodbye to be under the disapproving view of airport security."

Handing the keys to Daphne, I grab my suitcase, carry-on, and backpack from the back of the Escape and close the lift gate. With my baggage taken care of, I can give my girl the embrace she deserves. She lifts her lips to meet mine, wrapping her arms around my neck, and tunnels her fingers in my hair. Deepening our kiss, I stroke my tongue against hers and try to convey the love and desire I feel for her. I could do this forever, but I'm mindful of our limited time and the impending presence of airport security telling us to move along. Reluctantly, I pull back and gaze deeply into the face that owns my heart.

"I'm going to miss you, Daphne Foster, and you better be ready for me when I get home. Six weeks. Rest up."

Giggling, Daphne rests her hand on my heart and gives it a pat.

"You worry about yourself, Logan Morris. You better stay in shape these next six weeks. No getting all flabby with all the delicious food you're going to have. I have plans for you when you get home. I'll miss you too. We'll be okay."

With a grin and a flirtatious wiggle of her brows, she steps out of my arms and waits for a car to pass so she can get behind the wheel. I stand on the curb and motion for her to lower the window.

"Drive safely, Daphne. Six weeks. Forty-two days. Get ready."

"Get inside, Logan. The sooner you leave, the sooner you'll be home."

She blows me a kiss, and like a goof, I catch it and pretend to tuck it in my pocket. With a last wave, she pulls away from the curb and into the stream of traffic. I watch her go until I can't see her any longer. I want to tell her to come back. But what for? If she came back, I don't know if I'd tell her I love her, beg her to come with me, or something else, but I regret we left so much unsaid in our short time together.

With a frustrated sigh, I turn to enter the terminal and reluctantly start my journey.

25

DAPHNE

I HOLD ON TO MY COMPOSURE UNTIL I GET HOME. YEARS OF SUPPRESSING emotion for the win! I lost my parents tragically, and I will not dishonor their deaths by claiming dropping my boyfriend off at the airport was the hardest thing I've ever done, but this was hard because I had a choice this time.

"This is your fault," I tell myself. "You could have gone with him or asked him to stay."

I could see in Logan's expression that all I had to do was ask him not to go, and he'd be here with me in our home right this moment. But I'd worry he'd resent me and get bored being here. He enjoys traveling and doing new things. He said he doesn't want to be stagnant. Is that what I am? Stagnant like a murky pond with green scum on top? Why would anyone swim in a scummy pond?

I gaze around the living room. Other than the new couch, it's the way Gran left it after she passed. Same clock in the corner, same pictures on the walls, same ugly green carpet. Logan insisted I change the sofa. He borrowed his cousin's truck and dragged me to the IKEA in South Philly to buy this cute red couch. Gone is the floral monstrosity from the Ford administration that used to anchor the room. No more plastic seat covers, no stiff cushions, just comfort and color. I'm able to put my feet up on the cushions without guilt, something I never felt right doing on Gran's sofa. I've added my books to the shelves and a couple pictures of me and Logan, but it's mostly how it was when she was still alive. My home is like a calm, peaceful lake. No gigantic waves to capsize a canoe, no scary monsters under the surface waiting to drag you under. Is our home scummy and stagnant to Logan? Am I? Is that why I'm not worth staying with?

Walking into our bedroom, my bedroom, I see Logan left a couple of shirts behind for me. I tear up when I grab the green plaid flannel he wore yesterday. It smells like him. I think about putting it on, but then spy a stuffed moose Logan won for me at a carnival a few years ago and dress him in the shirt instead. This way, I can cuddle the moose, and the shirt won't have to be washed.

Taking off my sweater and jeans, I pull on the T-shirt Logan wore with his sleep pants this morning while we had breakfast. All I have left of the man I love is some dirty laundry. I never even told him I loved him. He thought I was asleep when he whispered he loved me in bed Friday night, but I heard him. Why didn't I tell him I loved him too? I thought I was protecting myself by keeping the words to myself because it would hurt more when he left me, but it hurts anyway, and now I don't have memories of us telling each other those precious words. What if something happens and I never get to look in his eyes and see his reaction when I tell him how I feel? If I see him again, no, *when* I see him again, I'll tell him I love him. In person. I'm not doing our *I love yous* over the phone or in a text. These are face-to-face words.

Taking a deep breath, I imagine my therapist, Claire, asking me if what I'm thinking is true, or if I'm falling into my habit of catastrophic thinking. I have been working hard to not let myself spiral when I get these thoughts. I may not be able to stop myself from thinking them, but I have the power to not let them overwhelm me.

"Okay," I tell myself, "I will take tonight to wallow, eat copious amounts of ice cream, and cry while watching Howlbark movies. I am not pond scum. Tomorrow is a new day. I will control what I can control. I am strong and will survive what I cannot control."

Grabbing my carton of Turkey Hill Chocolate Chip Cookie Dough ice cream and a spoon, I crawl into bed, turn on the TV, and scroll through my DVR to find a sickeningly sweet Howlbark movie to watch.

"Why is my pillow lumpy?" Sitting up, I feel around my pillow, and to my surprise, I discover a small box. There is a small, folded note taped on top.

I use my fingertip to open it and read out loud. "'Daph, I saw this and knew you had to have it. You have my heart, Logan.'"

I lift the lid off the basic white jewelry box. It's the wrong size and shape for a ring box, and I'm glad. If Logan was giving me a ring, then he damn well better be here putting it on my finger.

"Oh my gosh," I gasp. On a bed of cotton rests a delicate, open-work silver heart with a diamond in the center. It's from the Sunset Beach Gift Shop, so it's a Cape May diamond and not a genuine diamond, but that doesn't make it any less precious. I use the delicate silver chain strung through the heart to lift the necklace from its bed and hold it up to scrutinize it. The light catches the stone, causing it to sparkle. I love it. I want to put it on so I can feel it against my skin while I fall asleep, but I'm afraid I'll snap the dainty chain. I force myself to put it back in the box and wait for the morning to wear Logan's heart close to mine. Even if he isn't here with me in person, I still have something from him with me.

I'm not really alone.

Unless he gave me this as a goodbye present. Maybe he's not giving me his heart. Maybe this is just a trinket, and it doesn't mean anything.

I hit play and take my first spoonful of ice cream. Normally I savor the dough bits, letting them melt on my tongue, but this time I chomp through them.

I try to watch *A Winter Christmas Penguin Princess for a Reindeer Prince* without my interest being piqued. Okay, it wasn't named that, but they may as well have been. I decide to dip into my stash of non-winter movies and pick one about a city-slicker cougar shifter career woman traveling to the great outdoors to do something outside her comfort zone with a hunky wolf shifter outdoorsy guy offering sage advice and a chaste kiss an hour and fifty-five minutes in.

"Oh wow, it's a charmingly quirky blonde wandering the big city, bringing sunshine and light everywhere she goes. Ugh. I hate her." I roll my eyes but still watch the whole thing, smirking at their kiss five minutes before the end of the movie. This movie was great. I'll never admit it, but the scenario in the movie sparked an idea I'm eager to follow up on. As the credits roll, I grab the remote, stab it toward the TV, and hit the off button. I need to sleep anyway so I'm not a zombie at the office tomorrow.

The house is so quiet. It was just a week, but having Logan here, puttering around, making noise, and knowing I wasn't alone became my new normal. I miss it. I grab my moose and cuddle him close. I smell Logan on the shirt I dressed Mooster in. It's a comforting mix of his clean soap scent, our detergent, and Logan's basic aroma. I bury my nose in the shirt's collar and breathe deeply.

"Oh, Mooster. I don't think I can do this." After murmuring a prayer that Logan stays safe in his travels, I drift off to sleep.

"Mom?" I ask groggily. "What are you doing here?" I check my phone for the time—three in the morning, the witching hour.

"It seems like you need me, so I came to check on you," she answers.

"Okay...um, hi?" I don't know if I'm dreaming, if my mother's ghost is visiting, or if I'm going crazy. Maybe a combination of all three? Whatever it is, they look like my mom in her black-and-white striped T-shirt and jeans. If I look down, I'll probably see the black

Converse sneakers she loved to wear when not dressed in a suit and heels for the office. My parents were only thirty-six when they died. Now that I'm an adult, I realize how young that was. Her copper bob shows no signs of gray. She's still beautiful.

"Hi, honey. Gran and Dad send their love. Gran likes the couch."

"She does? I was afraid she'd be upset I got rid of her sofa."

"Daphne, she wants you to make this house your home or use it as your launch pad. She didn't intend for you to keep it as a shrine to the past when she left it to you. She wanted you to use it for your future. Keep it, sell it, whatever you need it for. Same for me and Dad. We never intended for you to become an accountant if that wasn't what you wanted. Yeah, we talked about you taking over Foster Accounting, but that was our dream, and we wanted you to have an easier path than we did. We would have been fine if you'd majored in something else or did the tour guide thing. We want you to be happy. Dad and I are worried about you."

I sit up with my back against the headboard.

Mom sits at the foot of my bed, just like she did when I was younger.

"You are? Why? Is something going to happen?" My heart beats faster. Is this visit a warning something bad is going to happen? Oh no. Logan. Am I going to lose him too? My breath comes in short pants. One of my anxiety attacks is coming on. I haven't had one in years.

"Daphne, breathe. In for four, hold for seven, out for eight. Come on, do it with me." Mom leads me through the breathing exercise, and I'm surprised she knows it. The attacks didn't start until after she died. As if she read my mind, she replies, "I've been with you in my own way. I'm so sorry you've gone through so much and felt alone. Dad and I didn't want to leave you. We would have stayed if we could have." She reaches out and holds my hand. It's warm and feels solid.

"I know. I've missed you both so much. I've been so alone." I swallow past the lump in my throat.

"No, you haven't. You've had Logan," Mom replies.

My gaze shoots up from where it was resting on our joined hands. "You know about Logan?"

"We do." Her lips curve into a wry smile I inherited from her. "It's about time you guys did something about it."

"What? How much do you see? Tell me Dad doesn't know. Oh my goodness, Gran!"

Mom lets out a hearty laugh. It's not genteel, like tinkling bells. It's more like an over-exuberant donkey. I've missed that laugh.

"Don't worry. You have your privacy. We have our own things to do, and we aren't watching you make out with your boyfriend." She shudders. "It's enough that I have to see your Gran and Pop make up for lost time. I don't need to see my little girl getting jiggy with it."

It's my turn to shudder. No one needs to hear their mother use the word "jiggy." Haven't I suffered enough? Oh my gosh, am I making a joke about losing my parents? What the hell is wrong with me?

"Nothing is wrong with you, Daphne. You're allowed to find humor and joy and be irreverent. It doesn't mean you don't miss us or didn't love us. That's why I'm here. We want you to be goofy and have fun and go on your adventures. Don't be afraid of the future. Embrace it. If there are bumps along the way, you'll deal with them. Plans shift. And so does your boyfriend. He's gorgeous as his eagle, by the way. You're strong and resilient. I think you've forgotten that, so I'm here to remind you. Don't waste your life being safe. That doesn't mean go out and be reckless. We're in no rush to have you join us." She laughs. "Sorry, couldn't help it."

A chuckle slips out. What else can I do? My mom is sitting here on my bed, holding my hand and making jokes about being dead. I'm not sure if I'm never eating chocolate chip cookie dough ice cream before bed again or eating it every night if this is going to happen.

"You know what I mean," she says. "Don't be reckless, but live your life. Fall in love, have a family, follow your dreams, go on adventures. Love is an adventure. It's the best adventure you can have."

My phone buzzes, and I reach over to see I have a text from Logan letting me know he arrived safely. It's just before seven in the morning now. I look around the room. "Mom?"

Silence. I'm alone.

Did I dream her visit, or was she really here? My boyfriend turns into a bird, so I don't think my dead mother visiting me is that outrageous in the big scheme of things. Whatever the truth is, she told me what I needed to hear.

"Thank you, Mom. I love you."

I never thought a Howlbark movie and a visit from my mother's ghost would offer the key to my future, but I guess stranger things have happened. Grabbing a pen, notepad, and my laptop, I make lists and google until it's time to get ready for work. I have the start of a plan, and I'll work on it more when I get home from work tonight.

26

LOGAN

It's been a long day. After landing in Madrid, I texted Daphne good morning and picked up my rental car to go to Marisol and Pierre's home, a lovely villa in Nueva España within the District of Chamartín, situated north of the city. I park my rented Mercedes and approach Marisol's door.

Before I can knock, the door swings open, and Pierre greets me with a hug and a warm smile. "Logan! Welcome! It has been too long. Mari is changing Ariana and will be down in a moment."

From behind Pierre, I hear, "Lolo!" A little black-haired missile rushes into my legs.

I bend to scoop him up. "Henri, I almost didn't recognize you. When did you start shaving?" I blow a raspberry against his cheek, making him giggle.

"Lolo, stop!" When I lower him to his feet, he grabs my hand, dragging me toward the salon. "¡Mira!"

He's pointing toward a black-painted rocking horse and tells me to look. He speaks a mishmash of Spanish, French, and English, depending which word comes to mind first. He understands all three languages. It's incredible. I can handle Spanish and French, but I'm not fluent, and Mari and Pierre have requested I speak English to Henri, partly to increase his familiarity with the language, but mostly so I don't confuse him with my poor grammar. I don't know what is normal for an almost three-year-old in terms of language skills, but Henri seems advanced. He climbs on the horse and starts rocking.

"What's its name?" I ask.

"Guillermo," he answers. All righty. I peek over at Pierre. He grins, shrugs, and shakes his head.

I hear steps approaching and turn to see a radiant Mari holding the prettiest baby I've ever seen.

"Ariana, meet your Lolo," she coos to her daughter, who gives a drooly, gummy smile in response. She has wispy dark blond hair and her mother's dark gaze and lashes. She's in a dark blue dress/shirt thing with blue-and-white striped footed pants underneath. Is it possible for a six-month-old to be fashionable? It must be because Ariana is like a little model. Henri is in brown corduroy pants with a green long-sleeved T-shirt, looking dapper too. I feel a bit rumpled and underdressed in the jeans and pullover I've been wearing since yesterday afternoon.

"Hello, Ariana," I say to the baby as I reach out to run a finger along her cheek. She grabs my finger in a powerful grip I wasn't expecting and tries to put it in her mouth.

With a laugh, Pierre rescues me by gently loosening her grip before she can start chewing. "She's teething, and everyone else's fingers are tastier than her own."

"Here, hold her." Mari hands Ariana to me. "I'll get her soother."

I smile at the bundle in my arms. "Hello, merry girl. I'm so happy to meet you." I glance at Pierre. "You're a very lucky man, my friend."

Smiling at his little girl, he runs a hand over her curls. "Oui, I am. How about you? Mari said you went home to visit your Daphne. Any progress?"

"Pierre, you didn't offer him anything to drink or tell him to take a seat," Mari says in admonishment. "I'm going to tell your mama you're a poor host!"

With a wry expression, Pierre extends his arm in invitation to sit on the sofa. I sit with Ariana on my lap. Mari hands her daughter a chilled teething ring she promptly puts in her mouth and starts gumming, making a nom-nom sound. Henri is content riding Guillermo while watching a Spanish cartoon.

"I started coffee. Did you sleep on your flight?" Mari glances around. "Where are your bags?"

I press a kiss to Ari's curls and breathe in her baby scent. She chooses that moment to let out a massive fart, and I am no longer smelling the sweet smell of baby soap and detergent. Instead, I'm engulfed in a cloud of something much more pungent. I think it even surprised the baby because her rosebud lips form an O shape, and then she giggles like it's the funniest joke ever.

"Come here, princess. Let's go check your diaper." Pierre extracts his giggling daughter from my grasp. "Sorry, she gets away with it because she's cute." He presses a kiss to her cheek and leaves the room.

"How can one little girl produce a smell so rank?" I ask.

Marisol laughs as she sets the coffee service on the table in front of the sofa and takes a seat in the armchair across from me. "Wait until you have your own children, Logan. Passed gas won't even make the top ten of the gross things you'll encounter in a day."

She pours coffee into the cups, its aroma wafting and helping to erase the stink bomb Ariana subjected us to.

"While we're on the subject of your children..." she says in her velvety Spanish accent.

"We aren't," I interject.

Mari ignores me and continues. "How are things with Daphne? She didn't come with you?"

I add cream and sugar to my coffee, knowing from experience that Mari's coffee needs to be diluted if I want any hope of sleeping in the next three days.

I take a sip and sigh. "No, she didn't come with me. She needs to renew her passport and has work. This all came up too suddenly for her to get away. She's not very spontaneous." I let out a huff of humorless laughter. "It's funny. I'm so go with the flow, and she's not, but we're perfect for each other."

Mari's bark of laughter was not what I was expecting.

"My dear, sweet, delusional man, you're one of the least *go with the flow* people I know. You give the impression of being a vagabond, going wherever the wind takes you, but you've planned everything out, and if your initial plan doesn't work, you move on to plans B through Q. You make it seem effortless and spontaneous, but you couldn't be as successful as you are without having things planned."

I'm not sure how to respond. She's not wrong. I do plan things, but that's being responsible.

"You're able to be...spontaneous...because you don't have any responsibilities." She stops me before I can react. "Logan, I love you, so I'm going to tell you the truth, even though you don't want to hear it." She takes a sip of coffee.

I decide to take one too, in part to brace myself, but also so I have something in my hands to anchor me. I nod for her to continue but lean forward with my forearms resting on my thighs, braced to defend myself.

She places her cup on the table and gently puts a hand on my arm, oblivious to my defensive position. Or trying to break it down.

"I'm not saying you're a wastrel. You work, you're responsible, but if you decided tomorrow you didn't want to be a travel photographer, you could quit and not destroy your world. From what you've told me, you don't have a car payment, you don't pay rent—ah ah ah." She gives me an admonishing glare when I go to interrupt her. "Yes, you pay Daphne, but it's not the same as having a mortgage and utilities. If you weren't living with her, you could live with your parents until you were ready to move some-where else. Your parents carry your health insurance. You have your trust fund Pierre invests for you. You have parents and grandparents and a brother who all love you and support you. You're very fortunate."

The breath I was holding wooshes out. I guess I was afraid what she was going to say would hit too close to home. It did.

"Daphne doesn't have any of that. She has you. She doesn't have a family. She doesn't have a safety net. She needs her job to have insurance, she has a house to support, and she needs to support herself. Even if she wanted to run away with you, and I'm sure she does, she can't do it without planning things to make sure she's covered her responsibilities and that if something happened, she could survive it financially and emotionally."

I'm ashamed I didn't consider all that. Of course, I would take care of Daphne, practically with things like health insurance, but also emotionally. If, God forbid, something happened to me, I'd make sure she was provided for. I can understand her caution. Her life was turned upside down when her parents died. Gran's death wasn't necessarily a surprise, but it always feels like it's too soon when a loved one passes. My dear, sweet Daphne. All I want to do is make her happy and make sure she feels safe, secure, and loved.

"I'm such a jerk," I moan to Marisol.

"Lolo jerk!" Sure, now Henri is paying attention to us.

Mari has become an expert at giving the mom look while saying her child's name. It's apparently an international skill, so my buddy goes back to rocking and watching his show.

Mari pats my shoulder. "You're not a jerk, Logan. You're just clueless. You can fix that. Idiocy can be overcome. Heartlessness cannot."

The sounds of happy baby babbles reach us when Pierre returns carrying a non-smelly Ariana.

"Let's try this again," I say, reaching for her. I place a kiss on her curls and tell her she's so much cuter when she doesn't smell like a sewer. Okay, I don't actually say she smelled like a sewer before, but it's implied. I balance her on my lap, hold her hands, and bounce my knees in an alternate rhythm like she's riding a horse. It makes her giggle, and I feel like I'm fulfilling my duties as an honorary uncle.

Henri decides he's done riding his rocking horse and comes over to climb on the couch next to me.

I stop bouncing Ariana, shifting her so she leans against my chest to enable me to put an arm around Henri when he cuddles into my side. I lean back on the couch and get comfortable because I assume I'll be here a while with a pair of sleeping kids using me for a pillow.

Pierre quirks a brow in silent question—do I want to be relieved of his children? I shake my head. Having these two sturdy little bodies against me feels oddly soothing.

Picking up our previously abandoned conversation, Marisol asks, "Where are your bags? Did you leave them in the car?"

"I'm staying in a hotel this time. I'll be talking to Daphne late in the evening, and I don't want to disrupt your family. But thanks for always making me feel welcome and offering your home to me."

Pierre chuckles. "What makes you think you won't have privacy to speak with your girlfriend? Our children wouldn't be waking you at the crack of dawn crawling into your bed or crying during the night. They only do that to us. Staying here is like staying at a hotel but without the privacy and room service."

His dry wit and obvious adoration of his wife and children are two of the things I most appreciate about Pierre. When Ariana soon follows her brother into nap time, I spend the couple of hours the kids are sleeping on me talking with their parents about my relationship with Daphne and my hopes for the future.

"I want to have what you two have one day—a loving marriage, happy children, knowing your partner is your person, and professional success. I truly believe Daphne and I can have that. We simply need to figure out how we can be in the same place at the same time and feel like we aren't giving up everything in order to make the other person happy."

I'm embarrassed to be twenty-six years old and just now having to compromise in a relationship. With past girlfriends, if we didn't want the same things, we'd part ways. Our feelings weren't deep enough to sacrifice for each other. I'm realizing that love isn't so much about sacrificing, but more about compromising. It shouldn't be one person giving up so the other person is happy. Instead, both people should work together so everyone is happy.

"I know I want to be with Daphne, and I'm willing to compromise to make sure we're together. By the same token, I'm self-aware enough to understand that, long-term, I need to still travel and experience new things. I like to be outdoors. I don't want to be in an office doing the same thing day in, day out. It would be so easy to work for my uncle and stay home to make Daphne happy, but I'm afraid I'll feel stifled and get frustrated."

Knowing Daphne like I do, she's probably having similar thoughts—traveling would be fun at first because it's new, but she wouldn't enjoy living out of a suitcase. She enjoys having a schedule and her own nest.

After the kids wake up from their naps, Pierre and I take them outside for some fresh air while Mari finishes up dinner. I kick a ball with Henri. Okay, I kick a ball and watch him run after it, my thoughts on what Marisol said about me and my situation.

She made me sound like I'm selfish and controlling. I'm not. Of course I plan. How do you get things done if you don't plan? There are people who just react to what happens and never make anything happen. Reactive versus proactive. That describes me and Daphne. She deals with the things that happen to her, but she rarely makes them happen. I'm all about making things happen. I don't want to be at the mercy of what the world throws at me. I want the world at my mercy. Let it adapt to me, not me adapt to it. Is that difference because of our basic personalities, or is it a human versus shifter thing? I'm a golden eagle shifter, the largest bird of prey in North America. Our kind is an apex predator, and we rule our skies.

In a romantic relationship, though, we can't be predator and prey. We need to be partners. It freaks me out she doesn't think about our future. That's all I think about. I'm certain we can have a glorious life together. Does she not see that? Can she *not* see that? Is she afraid to see that?

Henri carries the ball back to me, and I kick it again, sending him off giggling to chase it. Is Daphne afraid to think about our future because she doesn't trust it will come true? Is she afraid to plan for the future because she knows it can be taken away in an instant? That causes my heart to ache for her. I picture her like a shipwreck survivor being tossed in the ocean, clinging to a bit of debris and trying to stay afloat. Of course, she won't let go of it and take off swimming, hoping she'll find land. The life raft has to come to her.

I will be her life raft.

Pierre and I tidy up after we finish eating the delicious meal Mari prepared so she can enjoy a glass of wine. Henri is looking at a storybook and telling the story to Ari in French. It must be his favorite book because it sounds like he has it down pat, even making funny voices for the different animal characters like his parents must do.

Mari gives me a kiss on the cheek as I prepare to leave their home to go to my hotel. "I'm so happy to see you, Logan. It has been too long. Next time, bring Daphne."

"I'll do my best, Marisol. You know you can always visit us too." I shake Pierre's hand and pull him in for a hug. I already cuddled the kids and said my goodbyes to them. "It's not Madrid or Paris, but New Jersey has interesting things too."

"We're aware of that, Logan. We were waiting for you to realize it." Well, damn, there goes Mari dropping more truth bombs. "Yes, you're a travel photographer, but do you realize people travel to take pictures of what's in your own backyard? You don't have to travel all over the world to be successful." She shrugs. "If it's the photography that's important to you, there are plenty of subjects there. If it's the travel that's the focus and the photography is a way to support the travel, that's a different story. I guess it depends on what is important to you."

I hug her again and press a kiss to her cheek. "You're an excellent friend, Mari. Pierre, you're a lucky, lucky man."

Leaving their home, I drive to the historic hotel where I'm staying. It isn't as sleek and modern as many of the hotels in Madrid, but that is part of why I like it. I don't need all the bells and whistles and fitness centers. I'd rather have a place with character, and this place has that in spades. My room is clean, and the bed is incredibly comfortable. I take a shower to wash off the travel grime and crawl naked between the sheets. This feels incredible. Not as nice as my bed at home, but that's because Daphne isn't in it with me. I set three alarms on my phone, five minutes apart, starting at right before one in the morning so that I'm awake in time to call Daphne. It'll be seven in the evening for her, and she should be home from work and grocery shopping.

The five hours of sleep I'll get before speaking with her will hopefully erase the bags forming under my eyes. I'm not vain, but Daph will worry if I appear exhausted. I also know she finds me irresistible when I'm sleep-rumpled, and I always want to give my sunshine what she wants. And give her what she needs, even if she doesn't know she needs it.

Wait, that sounds controlling.

Now that Mari has called my attention to it, all I can think about is what a controlling ass I can be sometimes. That's the last thing I want to be with Daphne. I love her. I don't want to control her. I want us to work together for our goals and to find compromises for those times when our goals don't perfectly align. I feel part of these six weeks we're apart is going to be spent reading some self-help and relationship books. Because if I'm going to deserve Daphne and give her what she really needs, I need to learn a lot.

27

DAPHNE

"Good morning!" I call out, entering our area of the office.

Mallory is in the kitchen fixing a mug of cocoa.

"Good morning. Aren't you cute? I love the red shoes! Are you doing okay?"

"Thanks. I went spelunking in my closet." I grab my mug and fill it with hot water, leaning my hip against the counter while I unwrap my tea bag and drop it in. "I'm okay. Logan arrived in Madrid safely."

Grabbing a stirrer, sweetener, and a paper towel, I pick up my mug and walk to my desk.

"I apologize in advance if I'm mopey or grumpy. I also apologize for constantly saying, 'It's only five weeks. We got this.' It's my mantra. I guess it's my version of *fake it until you make it.*"

Mallory smiles. "You do you, boo. It sucks to be apart. I can't do it." She stirs her cocoa to get the powder mix to dissolve. "But the sex when you're back together is going to be awesome." She blows on her cocoa and takes a cautious sip. "Welcome home sex is stellar." She grimaces. "Well, it is when you've both been abstaining while separated. When you find out you're the only one who has been celibate while he's gone because he caught an STI while away...it sucks."

I have a feeling that's a story Mallory needs to share over a box of wine. She must see the expression of horror on my face because she laughs.

"Don't worry. That won't happen to you guys. Logan is crazy for you. He's one of the good guys."

That reminds me. "Did you want to grab lunch together today? We haven't done that in a while, and there's stuff I want to talk about. But not in the office."

It must intrigue her because her brows quirk up, and she smirks.

"Sure. Francisco's?"

She names the local pizza place down the road. They have excellent salads, so I can try to undo all the cheese I ate yesterday.

I nod. With lunch settled, we both log in to our computers and start working through our tasks for the morning. It's the end of the month, so I'm inundated with payoff requests for people selling their condos and preparing those forms for the title companies. Yay. I didn't need my degree in accounting to do this. I'm grateful for this job. I'm paid well. The benefits are great, and it isn't difficult. It's just boring. That was what I wanted at the time—stability and predictability. I didn't want to be challenged.

But now I'm feeling differently and wanting more than safety and a small life. Now I need to figure out how I'm going to get it.

"My car or yours?" Mallory asks as we grab our purses and exit the office. She drives a cute green Mini Cooper.

"Yours," I decide.

We ride the couple of miles to Francisco's. After ordering at the counter, each having decided on a chicken Caesar salad, we choose a booth along the far wall.

Mallory takes a sip of her Sprite and asks, "So, what's up? You had something you wanted to talk about?"

Our server, Lindsey, drops off a basket of warm Italian bread, and I busy myself buttering a slice before answering.

"Yeah, I do." It's silly I'm nervous, but I am. "I'm going to ask to cut my hours to part-time in the new year, and I want to take vacation time the week of Thanksgiving."

Lindsey delivers our salads, and we smile our thanks up at her.

"I didn't know if you were hoping to take any time off for the holidays. If you were, I wanted to coordinate it, so we both get the time we want."

Unwrapping her silverware, Mallory replies, "I'm flying to visit my parents for Thanksgiving, but I plan to leave on Wednesday afternoon. You being gone won't impact that."

She uses her fork to stir the salad and distribute the dressing.

"I'm going to cash out most of my vacation time. You know you can do whatever you want. You don't have to clear things with me."

I nod, chewing my first bite of salad. I wish it was a cheeseburger.

She loads her fork with chicken and lettuce. "I think it's great you're taking time off. I hope you're planning on traveling with Logan."

I shrug. "I know I don't need your permission to adjust my hours, but it could affect you, so I wanted to give you a heads-up. I don't know if more work would fall in your lap, or if they'd just close the department. I sometimes think they have things as they are so there's a spot for me to work. I know they hired me because of my connection to Logan. I was essentially a pity hire. I appreciate it, it's what I needed at the time, but it's not right for me. I didn't want to blindside you." I take a sip of my iced tea. "I still need to work out how much I'm comfortable traveling with Logan. I need the health insurance and other benefits, so I need to work enough hours to keep my benefit status."

Swallowing her bite of salad, Mallory wipes her mouth. "Daphne, you're very sweet, but seriously, don't worry about me. I'll be fine whatever happens. I can get another job pretty easily. I have law firms reach out to recruit me all the time." She takes a sip of her soda. "If they closed our department, they'd most likely offer us positions in another department. They would welcome you in payroll or accounting if you wanted. They hired me to work in leasing. I'm in collections only because George and Martha were retiring, and it was easy to slot me in there. I don't think they'd lay either of us off. We're outstanding employees." She grins. "I stay because it's a reasonably easy, well-paying job, and I have the best coworker."

I smile back at her. "I definitely lucked out having you for my dungeon mate this past year, Mallory. Thanks for not freaking out." I decide to press my luck. "Do you have plans for Saturday afternoon?" I caught her mid-bite.

She holds up a finger in the universal sign for *wait a minute,* and then she replies. "No. Saturday I was planning on hanging at home doing laundry and bingeing Netflix. Sunday morning, I'm meeting my girls for breakfast. You're welcome to join us. Why?"

"So I want to try filming a tour out at the wildlife refuge. Wear a head-mounted camera so the viewers see things from my point of view and hear me talk about what I'm seeing. I spent hours last night watching different tours on YouTube, and it's so cool. I've always wanted to be a tour guide, and this is a new twenty-first-century way of doing it. There are portals you can sign up with to be hired to give live virtual tours to people who reserve them. You can upload pre-recorded tours and have them available to rent. Or you can stream them on YouTube, maybe get monetized if you have enough viewers, get tipped via pay apps, set up a merchandise shop with T-shirts and mugs. There are tons of things you could do with it. I can handle the filming and editing, my friend Shelby has equipment to loan me and has given me some tips, but I'll feel awkward walking through the woods alone, talking to myself. If you're there, I can talk to you and not feel like a goober."

"Oh, my goodness, that sounds so cool! I haven't been out to the refuge in forever. Count me in!"

With our plans made for Saturday, I shimmy in my seat and do a little clap of happiness. Anyone looking at me would think I was a dork. I don't care. This is the first step toward my future.

The rest of the workday passes quietly. I stop for groceries and enter my house. I was going to cook myself dinner, but I only have an hour before I connect with Logan, and there are a few things I want to do, so I picked up a spicy turkey club sandwich from Wawa on my way home. I sit at the breakfast bar with my laptop and take a bite of my sandwich while my computer wakes up. My passport sits on the counter in front of me. When I retrieved it from the fireproof box I keep my important papers in, I saw my parents' passports lying there, too. They had renewed them right before the accident, and they arrived a week after their funeral. They were looking forward to filling them up with stamps once I left for college, and they were going to visit me on whatever semester abroad program I chose. Their old passports only had a stamp from the trip to Jamaica they took when I was seven. It was their long-awaited honeymoon. They had gotten pregnant with me when they were in college, so had a small wedding and a weekend getaway honeymoon. Big weddings and grand honeymoons weren't options when you needed to pay your tuition for senior year and start saving for Pampers.

Once Foster Accounting was on solid ground and I was in school, they left me with Gran and Pops and took a week away. Seeing their new unstamped passports makes me sadder than looking at my own expired, unstamped passport. I only had one trip planned. I was going to go to Spain with my high school's Spanish club the summer between junior and senior years. That didn't happen. Just like all the trips Mom and Dad planned never happened. I lock away the sadness with the passports in the safe and pop open my computer, my ghost mom's reminder to live life to the fullest ringing in my mind.

"Okay, what do I need to do to renew my passport?" I google and fill out what I need to, splurging to get it renewed in an expedited manner and kicking myself for letting it expire. I should have started the renewal process months ago since it was due to expire in August, but I didn't. I wasn't going anywhere. There was no rush. I hate it when past me was an idiot.

I can't believe only two and a half weeks ago I was sitting on this couch with my phone and iPad, drinking my rum and Diet Pepsi, waiting for Logan to FaceTime me from Prague. So much has changed since then. We've snuggled and made out on this couch, we've cooked meals together in the kitchen, and we've slept together in our bed.

Nothing has really changed, though. I'm still working at a job that doesn't fulfill me, and he's still thousands of miles away, traveling and going on his adventures. I have ideas to change things so we can be together, and I'm hopeful Logan will support me.

The FaceTime notification shows up exactly at seven, and I click to connect. Logan's handsome face fills the screen. He is in bed with his chest bare and his hair rumpled. He must have slept before calling me.

"Hey, Sunshine. How was your day?" Oh my, Logan's voice is all deep and rumbly, and I feel it in my core.

I press my thighs together in reflex.

"It was good. I had lunch with Mallory, and we talked about work stuff." I take a deep breath and blurt out, "Would you be okay if I cut back to part-time after the new year? I need to know the minimum number of hours I need to keep my health insurance and make enough to cover my bills, but I think I can structure my schedule so I can travel with you a bit. I can't travel full-time, but I want to be with you."

My hands are shaking. I'm nervous. How will he respond? I clasp them and hold them in my lap so Logan can't see.

His large, radiant smile reassures me. "Daphne, yes! Absolutely! I love it. Have you spoken to Uncle Will?"

I guess he's good with the idea.

"I haven't spoken to him yet. I wanted to let Mallory know first since this will affect her. I don't know if my going part-time will be the impetus to close the department, or if they'd pile more work on her. They could lay us both off, but Mallory doubts that will happen. She figures they'll move us over to something else within the legal department. I don't think I'd like that, but I don't know what I'd want to do."

I'm rambling because I'm nervous, which is silly because this is Logan. I can tell him anything. He's wanted me to quit or cut back forever so I can travel with him. He's always wanted that. Gah, why am I nervous?

"Daph, breathe. It's okay. I know you're scared, but I got you." Logan's words are reassuring. But having him here with his arms around me would be even better.

"I know. It's scary. I haven't even done anything yet beyond talking to Mallory, but that felt like a commitment to changing, and you know I don't do change well."

"That's not true, sunshine. You've had so much change and upheaval in your life, and you've dealt with it. It makes sense to want to control the things you can when so much in your life has been out of your control."

I feel the prick of tears because he finally understands me. He's always been my friend and has accepted me for who I am, mostly, but I'm aware I frustrate him sometimes with my reluctance to jump into things. He never knew fearless, adventurous me. I thought she died when my parents did, but it turns out she only went into hibernation, and she's about to reawaken as an older, wiser, more cautious version of that girl. This version knows there are things to be cautious of but is not afraid because she's strong enough to deal with what comes her way.

The years since my parents' deaths may have tempered the fearlessness and sense of spontaneity I had as a girl, but they gave me strength and resiliency. I'm grateful for that. Finally. Accepting and understanding are two different things, and feeling understood is stirring unexpected feelings in me. We spent the past week exploring each other's bodies, but I think this is the most intimate with another person I've ever felt.

Sniffling, I choke out, "Oh, Logan, my heart. Oh, thank you for the necklace! I love it! It's beautiful."

When he sees my tears, an expression of alarm crosses his face.

I giggle. My tears are his kryptonite. It's a weapon I'm careful not to use against him. "I'm okay. Don't worry. I'm happy. How was your day? You spent time with Mari?" It's easier to change the subject than delve into my feelings tonight. "I hope you got pictures of the kids."

Going along with my change of subject, Logan replies, "I did. I'll send them in the morning. Mari sends her love."

I smile. I've never met Marisol in person, but we've texted and chatted a few times. I know she and Logan were never lovers, but I sometimes still feel insecure about their friendship. Mari is deeply in love with her husband though, and even if she wasn't, there isn't a romantic spark between her and Logan.

She's his very good friend, and I'm glad they're friends. I was jealous for a while because it appeared that she had everything I'd never have, but I got over that years ago. I have something she'll never have—Logan's heart.

It's the middle of the night for him, so I don't intend on keeping him on the phone too late.

"Were you leaving Madrid tomorrow? Well, in the morning, I guess. For you. It's already tomorrow there."

"I am leaving Madrid in the morning and starting the drive to Lisbon, and then I'm going to Golegã for the Feira Nacional do Cavalo." I love the accent he uses to pronounce that. "The Portuguese National Horse Fair." Logan knows I've always loved horses. I wish I was going with him, but there will be other years. "There are equestrian competitions in show jumping, dressage, driving, and other disciplines and cultural events like art exhibits and photography showcases." He shifts in bed, and I enjoy watching his muscles flex. "Have you ever gone to the Devon Horse Show?"

From Portugal to Pennsylvania, that's a leap. "Nope, have you?"

He shakes his head. "No. We should go next year. I think it's in May?"

I can't help my grin because he's planning on being here in May. "I'd love that."

Logan yawns, and I glance at the clock over the TV. It's almost half past one in the morning there. He must be tired. Even though he slept on the plane, today was a long day, and his body is off schedule.

"How far is the drive?" I ask Logan. "Can you do it in one day?" I can find Madrid and Lisbon on a map and judge the distance in miles, but that doesn't tell me how long the drive truly is. I don't know what the highway system is like, the speed limits, or if there are places he'll want to stop at along the way.

"It's about four hundred miles to Lisbon, and if I drove straight there, it would be about a seven-hour drive. I could easily do it in one day, but I will most likely take two days. There are a few places I've read about that I want to explore." He yawns again.

"Honey," I say, "go back to sleep. I want you well-rested for your drive tomorrow. Text me whenever you want, and we'll figure out when to talk next. With my work schedule and the time difference, we'll have to figure out when we can talk without exhausting each other."

"I'm sorry, sunshine," Logan says through a jaw-cracking yawn. "I want to spend time with you. I imagined me being propped up on the couch next to you watching TV through your iPad, but I'm beat."

I think he means he'll stay on FaceTime while I point my tablet at the television so we can watch the same show at the same time. But who the heck knows?

"It's okay, Logan. We'll figure this out. Sleep well and dream of me." I blow him a kiss, and he makes a kissy face back to me. We tell each other goodbye and other mushy things and disconnect.

Grabbing a pen and paper, I write lists of what I want to do and the steps I need to take to get it done. I don't know if it's an accounting thing or a trait I picked up from my parents, but I love writing lists, developing budgets, and making sure things balance. Having a plan in writing and the steps I need to take to carry them out broken down so I can check them off makes my little control freak heart happy.

"Thanks, Mom and Dad," I say to the empty room. I get a whiff of the aftershave Dad used to wear, but it's fleeting. Maybe I imagined it, but I'm choosing to take it as an acknowledgment of my thanks and a gesture of support.

"All righty, I've taken care of what I can do tonight. Time to relax with my knitting and watch some rugby."

Even knowing the outcome of the matches, I like to watch my recordings. They're good company in my quiet house. Plus, rugby thighs. I first became a fan of rugby watching Logan play for the club team at our university. I started attending matches to support him, but soon the pace and excitement of the game caught my attention. Okay, so did thirty guys in shorts. But I'm not the rugby equivalent of a puck bunny or jersey chaser. Ruck bunny? I don't know what they call them, but I'm not one.

Would Logan like to go to a professional rugby match with me?

Time to start a new list—adventures I want to take.

As I write, I decide to do two lists: one for things in North America and the other list for adventures overseas. Of course, my lists end up morphing into Google searches and bookmark collections. Ideas are coming at me in a flood, and I record notes on my phone using the dictation feature. I sign up for travel guides and newsletters. I watch so many YouTube videos.

"Ooh, this is so cool," I gush as I click play on the next one. I can't wait to share my ideas with Logan. Realizing it's almost midnight, I close my laptop and get ready for bed. I shoot a little video of me and Mooster in bed telling Logan goodnight.

I smile as I settle into bed and turn on the TV, hoping *Murder, She Wrote* will lull me to sleep. I can't wait for the weekend. If the weather cooperates, my plan is workable. My final thought before I drift off to sleep is that I should add visiting the places where Jessica Fletcher has solved murders to my list of adventures. She's traveled all around the world, and someday soon, I will too.

28
LOGAN

IF I CAN'T WAKE UP WITH DAPHNE IN MY ARMS, I GUESS WAKING UP TO HER sweet message on my phone is the next best thing. For the first time, I really don't want to be here. I don't want to be going somewhere new either. I want to be home with Daphne. It's weird being homesick. Of course, I've missed my family and Daphne while I've been away before, but the lure of excitement and adventure has always been stronger than my longing for them. FaceTiming or texting had always been enough contact to fulfill any need I had to connect with people at home. This time it's not. I have things to do this trip. I can't pick up and leave because I want to kiss my girlfriend. I really want to though, so it's a struggle to get out of bed, do what I need to check out of the hotel, and hit the road to travel to my next destination.

I give my best impression of a grown man and do what I need to, stopping at a café for a croissant with ham and melted cheese accompanied by a cup of coffee en route to Mérida, a town about three and a half hours southwest of Madrid. It's an ancient Roman city that holds many incredible ruins, dating back over two thousand years.

I decide to spend the night at one of the historic hotels in town and take pictures of the old Roman architectural details and text them to Daphne while I eat dinner. She loves these kinds of things. And I thank God for it. An architecture history class is where we met, after all.

I can't imagine my life without her in it. I'm not expecting a response to my texted pictures since she's still at work, so it is a pleasant surprise when my phone dings.

> Daphne: Oh wow, that's gorgeous. It was a convent? Is it haunted?

> Me: If any place is haunted, I would assume this would be. It's built on the site of an ancient Roman temple. There are artifacts from the Romans, Visigoths, and Moors here. It's incredible.

> Daphne: Wow, I can't imagine seeing sights that are over 2000 years old.

> Me: We can visit them someday. Are you still at work?

> Daphne: Yeah, I need to finish up some payoffs for the end-of-the-month closings. Are you going to bed soon?

> Me: I should. I loved your message, the second-best thing to waking up to you in person.

> Daphne: Oh good. I guess we're going to have to schedule our FaceTime because of the time difference and my job. You can't stay up late every night waiting for me to get home from work. We can do morning your time and I'll stay up late. We probably can't talk every day.

> Me: Why can't we? We'll figure it out. Even if it's a quick 'tell me about your day' sort of thing, I want to see and hear you.

A FaceTime invitation from Daphne appears on my screen. Swiping to accept, I can feel my heart beating faster. Daphne's beautiful face fills my phone screen, and I can see the shelves of files behind her. It's dark down there. It must be dreary to be stuck in a space like that without windows or natural light, surrounded by dusty files. I'd hate it.

But her sunny smile lights up the office-shaped shadows like a summer afternoon. "Hey, you! How's your day?" I can hear Mallory in the background making kissy noises.

Daphne giggles and flips her the bird. If she must be in the dungeon, at least she likes her cellmate.

"Hello, sunshine," I say. "My day has been okay. How about you?"

"He calls you sunshine? Oh my God, Daphne, that is the sweetest thing I've ever heard! I want to be a bridesmaid!" I guess this is a conversation for three since Mallory is joining in.

"It's okay. I'm stuck working with a crazy person, but it could be worse. We're dealing with the usual end-of-month busyness."

"You know you love me!" Mallory's cheeky grin appears over Daphne's shoulder, and she peers into the screen. "Do you have a brother?"

She cracks me up. "Yeah, but he's still in college, gay, and not as awesome as I am."

"I can work with all that!" I hear a beep, and Daphne makes an *oh shit* face.

Mallory calls out, "Hi, Will!"

My uncle must have come to their area. How much did he hear?

"I'll let you go. Talk later," I tell Daphne as she nods and blows a kiss before signing off.

I hope they aren't in trouble. Uncle Will is cool and won't punish them for being goofy. But she's concerned about things being awkward now that we're in a relationship and she's like family. She *is* family. She's the person I want to make a family with.

And I want to be with my family. And not just through a screen someone can easily turn off. But instead, tomorrow, I'll continue my drive to Portugal. Another town, another festival, another day, oceans away from the only person I really want to be around right now.

As I eat the steak I ordered for dinner, I think about how I can take care of the things I need to do in the shortest amount of time. I have a plan, but I think I need to revise it. When I get back to my room, I open my laptop and research other Christmas markets.

"Okay, what markets open earliest?" I mutter to myself, tapping away on my laptop. My intention was to attend the major markets that start in late November, covering the classic markets in Germany and Austria. My research shows me that there are markets in Manchester, England and Edinburgh, Scotland that start earlier in November. I could cover those, and then there are three in eastern France and western Germany opening within a few days of each other a little later in November. I could finish what I need to do and make it home in time for Thanksgiving. I imagine Daphne's surprise if I showed up weeks early.

Chuckling to myself, I shake my head. Mari has me pegged. I am a planner.

29

DAPHNE

It's rare that the big boss comes down to our area. On the few occasions we need to discuss things with Will, we do it in his office. I think he knows I was speaking with his nephew, but he doesn't seem to care.

"Hey," he says, "just checking in to see how you're doing down here. Swamped with end-of-month stuff?" Will glances around our space and seems to be disturbed by what he sees. "It is really dark down here."

Mallory and I glance at each other.

She answers, "No, we're good. What's up?" Since we don't get visitors here, there aren't extra chairs, but that's not an issue for Will. He sits on top of a spare desk that got schlepped down here when it was deemed unworthy of being upstairs. Yes, our area is where old office furniture goes to die.

"Nothing, really. You two are in your own little world down here, and I'm nosy." We all laugh.

Mallory and I glance at each other. She gives me a look that's clearly a question. *Have I spoken to Will about my plans already?* I shake my head slightly to show that I haven't.

"I'll let you get back to work," Will says. "My door is always open if you need anything." Will rises from the desk he's been sitting on.

Why is he here? Does he know something? Did Logan tell him something? I want to think he wouldn't because it's for me to tell, but sometimes he thinks he knows what's best and butts in where he shouldn't. I hope he didn't.

"Cool, thanks, Will," I say.

"Bye, Will," Mallory adds.

Our gazes meet as the door beeps, signaling Will's exit.

"Was that weird?" I ask.

"A bit. Do you think he knows you want to cut back?"

"I don't know. I spoke to Logan about it last night, and I hope he wouldn't interfere, but he's a goober sometimes."

Mallory rises from her desk and heads to our kitchen area. "I need a double cocoa with extra marshmallows. Want one?"

That sounds scrumptious, so I grab my mug and follow her. I decide to walk on the wild side and add a touch of French vanilla powdered creamer to mine.

"Ooh, good idea," Mallory enthuses. "Ooh, do you think they make peppermint creamer? That would be yummy in the cocoa."

Nodding, I say, "We should ask Betty to check when she's ordering the coffee supplies." "Speaking of orders, did you have what we need for Saturday?"

"Yep. I borrowed a camera that can mount on a head strap and a microphone. The strap will arrive tomorrow, and I borrowed the camera and microphone from Shelby. The weather forecast says it will be good for Saturday. Her boyfriend, Finn, is a Fish and Wildlife Services officer based at the refuge, and he's told me some interesting things about the trail I'll incorporate into my tour." I dump a handful of marshmallows into my cocoa. "Thank you so much for being willing to do this with me, Mallory. I've been researching and watching other online tours around the world, but I haven't found anything recorded locally. New Jersey is the butt of a lot of jokes, but there are so many wonderful things here that I want to share with the world."

She smiles at me. "Daphne, it sounds like fun. Thanks for asking me. When you're famous and have your own show on the Travel Channel or you're a contestant on *Dancing with the Stars* because you're a social media influencer, I expect to be introduced to your famous friends and offered tickets to tapings."

I don't want to be famous, and dancing alongside minor celebrities sounds like hell. All I want is a new gig, a lot of time with Logan, and a bit of freedom. This idea that is quickly turning into a new dream—the first dream I've had in years—could do just that. This time, I'm going to hope for the best instead of imagining the worst.

———————

Logan and I have worked out a schedule of texting, leaving each other voice messages, and FaceTiming when our schedules sync. He is in Golegã, Portugal at the National Horse Fair. All week he's been sending me samples of the pictures he's been taking, and they're gorgeous. Action shots from the show jumping and dressage competitions, scenic pictures of the area, portraits of the horses—they're all wonderful.

The practice tour Mallory and I did at the wildlife refuge went well. We walked a short eco trail loop that offered a splendid view of the Atlantic City skyline, the bay, and looped through a wooded area. The refuge is on a major migratory bird route, so there's a ton of different varieties of birds to see. In early November, it's Canada geese, snow geese, cormorants, ducks, and seagulls. There are always seagulls, but you never see *baby* seagulls. It's odd; if you visit in the spring, you'll see goslings and ducklings but no baby gulls. I think they fly up from the bowels of hell fully grown. Damn devil birds.

I've been editing the video after work this week. We did the loop three times to get as much footage as possible. Since I'm wearing a head-mounted camera, I filmed everything from my point of view, so

I had to make sure I was describing what I was seeing and not observing one thing while talking about another.

"And we're live!" My hands are trembling slightly as I hit the keys necessary to upload my video. I add links to my social media accounts to get a few views, hopefully. Shelby is a popular social media influencer with hundreds of thousands of followers, so she's sharing links too on her platforms.

"Shared!" Shelby says.

Mallory and Shelby have come over to cheer me on, drink wine, and Mallory is going to crash in the guest room. Her parents live in Florida, and she bought the family home from them. They came back up north to attend a family party, announced they were staying with her, and are driving her crazy. She was afraid to admit that to me since I lost my parents, but I get it. I loved my parents, and we were close, but we had our moments where we got on each other's nerves. I can't imagine having a relationship with them as an adult, especially if they came into my home and treated it like it was still their house and acted like I was still a child and not a grown woman. Shelby's boyfriend is going to pick her up and take her back to his house a couple of miles away.

Shelby and I joined Mallory for brunch on Sunday morning with her girlfriends, and it was a lot of fun. I made a promise to myself to not let these new friendships fade once Logan comes home in just over four weeks. It would be so easy to immerse myself in our relationship to the exclusion of everyone else, and I don't want to be the girl that ignores her female friends when her boyfriend is available. I want to have a balance between my romantic relationship and my friendships.

"Time for wine," Mallory states, and she opens the cans of rosé so we can kick back on the couch to watch a few fall-themed Howlbark movies. Mallory comes from a family of wolf shifters, and Shelby is human like I am, but her boyfriend is a Bigfoot shifter, so we enjoy the shifter romance movies. It's funny how they're formulaic like the regular Hallmark movies with the shifters being seen in their other form and stirring feelings in the others. They usually do shifter/human pairs so there's the *oh no, we're so different* moments of doubt until we get to the *no matter what form we shift into, we're all the same deep down inside* moment of realization before the declarations of love. It's hokey, but it's what I need right now. We're ready to relax and pig out with our mini buffet of cupcakes, leftover Halloween candy, chips, cheese and crackers, and bottles of water on the coffee table in front of us. I grabbed fleece blankets so we can be cozy while we binge. I haven't had a slumber party with girlfriends since before my parents died, and this is fun, especially with the addition of wine. I've never had canned wine before. I'm surprised at how tasty it is. There's a lot of things I've never done before, but I'm going to. No more being hide-in-the-shadows Daphne. It's time for me to embrace the adventurous side of me that I've buried for the past decade. Time to embrace a lot of things. And Logan.

30
LOGAN

It takes a moment for me to remember where I am before I start my day. I know I'm not home with Daphne, but that's where I want to be.

"Why did I think I wanted to do all these festivals this month?" I groan, rolling to my side to take in the view out the window. "This sucks."

I'm doing this because it will enable me to sell many of the pictures I take to publications, companies, and websites immediately. The photos not snapped up with exclusive licenses I can put on stock photo sites for use on blogs or book covers. I'm also researching uploading images to an online portal that allows them to be printed on surfaces like mugs, pillows, shirts, whatever people want. I want to have my photos create an income for us without having to travel constantly. My family is wealthy, and Andy and I and our cousins have trust funds. Liam and I are old enough to access the funds, but we both plan on leaving them to grow for the future. Pierre has invested some of mine. I could support us on my trust fund, but we were raised to work and have careers. I want to be able to earn enough with my photography to be able to support Daphne and our family. Maybe this way, I can have a future with Daphne, with us both in the same hemisphere more often than not, ideally in the same bed.

I feel the call of nature, so I get my butt out of bed and enter the bathroom. The tile work is busier than my style, but I like the color combination of shades of tan and green. The bathroom attached to our bedroom back home could use an update. I think I'll suggest this color combo to Daphne.

"Dude, you look like crap," I tell my reflection while I wash my hands. I haven't been sleeping well. One week of sharing a bed with Daphne has ruined me for sleeping alone. I've never felt like I couldn't sleep without someone in bed beside me before. Other than Daphne, I haven't shared a bed with anyone since my few flings in college, and that wasn't the same. I grab my phone off the nightstand and unlock it to see if there are any new texts from Daphne. My heart sinks. No texts. Even though we messaged last night before I turned in. Now that it's the weekend, we should be able to FaceTime more. I'm eager to see her face.

"What's this?" I click on the notification that Daphne has posted a video. It's public, so I'm praying she didn't post something personal by accident. We've been sending each other flirty videos that are progressively getting hotter. Clicking the link, I see Daphne's smiling face, and I can't help but smile in response. She's outside, but I'm uncertain where.

"Hi! I'm Daphne, and today I'm going to share with you the Eco Trail at the Wildlife Refuge in Shifting Pines, New Jersey. I hope you enjoy experiencing this how I see it. If you'd like to be notified when I upload future tours, be sure to give me a thumbs up below and follow the link to sign up for my email newsletter to get more information on the places we explore." The view then switches to what Daphne sees. She must be wearing a head-mounted camera. Where'd she get that?

She steps onto the trail and starts speaking. "The Eco Trail is right past the visitor center and before the start of Wildlife Drive. It straddles marshland and forest. If you're at the refuge in the warmer months, beware that it is very buggy, with mosquitoes, gnats, and greenhead flies. It's November now, so bugs aren't much of an issue, thank goodness. You'll always want to take precautions against ticks. This trail has two paths. First, we'll follow the boardwalk along the marsh. In the distance, across Reeds Bay, you can see the skyline of Atlantic City. Yes, this gem of nature is just miles away from the casinos of Atlantic City." She walks both forks of the trail, explaining what she sees, pointing out flora and fauna, reminiscing how she used to walk these trails with her parents, pointing out a plank she purchased as part of a fundraiser for the refuge and had engraved with her parents' names as part of the boardwalk.

I didn't know she'd done that.

"Wow, Daph, you're doing it," I murmur, my eyes glued to the video. She's so warm and personable, it feels like I'm there with her. I've never walked this trail or flown over this part of the wildlife refuge, but she's being so descriptive and informative, it's easy to imagine what it's like. She also lets nature speak. She doesn't feel the need to chatter constantly, so I can hear the leaves rustling and bird-song. I like that she doesn't pretend to be an expert. She admits when she sees a bird she can't identify and encourages viewers to share their best guesses in the comments. I'm so proud of her. I know she doesn't enjoy being on camera, but she worked out a way to do it without that being necessary. I'm assuming she had company— probably Mallory—because I can't imagine she'd walk around talking to herself. She gave a tour, just like she always dreamed of doing. I feel the sting of tears, and my throat tightens. If she could do this by herself, I can imagine how great she'd do if she had a group to lead and interact with. She posted the video last night, and it has a couple hundred views so far. I'm sure her friend Shelby is helping spread the word.

"Let's get you more viewers, sunshine," I say as I share the video on my personal social media and in a few photography and tourism groups I'm in. This deserves to be seen by as many people as possible. It's the middle of the night for Daphne, so I don't message her. I grab a notepad from my carry-on and discover the envelope that arrived in the mail the day I left home. I'd forgotten all about it. It's a flyer for a photo tourism company in Michigan. They must have bought a mailing list from a photography supply business because I've never heard of them. Their flyer isn't that good, but they have a website, and I have free time, so I grab my laptop and check it out.

They offer classes to teach people how to use photo editing software and how to use their cameras. I'm not their target audience. I already know that stuff.

"Hell, I could teach these classes," I mutter to myself.

I scroll further down the page and see that they host photo retreats. Intrigued, I click and am taken to a page showing pictures of Michigan lighthouses, a few wildlife shots, and landscapes. They take groups of photographers to these sites for photographic opportunities and then help them edit their shots to achieve the best images possible. Hmm.

There's a nice selection for breakfast. I think. Truthfully, I barely notice the food, though I eat. I'm writing furiously in my notebook—things to research, questions, ideas. I have a lot of things to investigate and consider, but I think a photo tourism business back home in New Jersey could be successful. There is so much in the area that would make a great subject—the lighthouses Daphne visited, wildlife at the refuge and in the Pine Barrens, houses in Cape May, the ocean. Just sitting here, I thought of five tours I could do. Even a tour for shifters because we'd be able to access areas difficult for humans to reach. There are gear bags specially developed for shifters so they can shift, carry their equipment, and shift back to human form to take the shot. Since I'm an eagle shifter, I can get a literal bird's-eye view.

Could I use that to help Daphne with her videos? I probably look crazy with my mad scribbling and mumbling to myself, but I'm excited. If I can get this off the ground—I snort-laugh at my unintended pun—I'll be well on the way to setting up the life I want to have with the woman I love.

31
DAPHNE

I WONDER WHO HAD TWENTY-FIVE DAYS IN THE FAMILY BETTING POOL OF how long Logan and I could stand to be apart? I kept up the mantra of X more weeks. We can do this. And I believe it. But I don't want to wait another three weeks to be with Logan again. I'm flying to Paris. My trip is a surprise to Logan. Liam and Will promised not to tell him. They only know of my plan because, well, I work for Will, and Liam drove me to the Newark airport yesterday afternoon.

When I requested my time off, I spoke to Mike about wanting to cut back my hours in the new year. I explained how I was doing video tours and wanted more time to devote to that. It turns out he had seen the two tours I'd done so far, thanks to Logan sharing the links. Our discussion turned to the minor in marketing I'd earned in college and how videos showing the outlet centers could be excellent marketing tools. We brainstormed with Will and came up with the idea of doing video tours of the area around the outlets and coordinating with local attractions for joint marketing. We're going to test-drive it using the local centers, but if they're successful, it may be something we take nationwide. I don't know how Logan is going to react when I tell him. Hopefully, he's understanding that I don't want to just tag along on his adventures. I want to have adventures of my own. He can come with me if he wants.

I worked half a day on Friday so I could make my nonstop flight to Paris. If I flew out of Philly, I'd have layovers, and I wouldn't arrive in Paris until Saturday afternoon after flying over twelve hours. By flying from Newark, I arrive shortly after seven in the morning local time and my flight is merely seven hours. I owe Liam big-time.

This week, Logan has been in Paris attending markets that opened early. Later this afternoon, his plan is to travel to Strasbourg, a city a couple of hours east of Paris when traveling by train. My plan is to text him when I land and figure out how to get where he is. If he's already left for Strasbourg, then I'll take the train to meet him. I just crossed the Atlantic Ocean, so a two-hour train ride isn't a big deal, especially when we're at least in the same country again!

I heed the announcement to return my tray to the upright position. We must be landing soon. I can't believe I'm doing this. It's the most spontaneous thing I've ever done. Okay, it wasn't truly spontaneous. I had to renew my passport and order plane tickets—those things required planning. But this is spontaneity, Daphne Foster style. Normally, I would've planned for months, with multiple to-do lists and lists of pros and cons, and, in the end, I would've talked myself out of doing it.

I'm proud of myself. To anyone else, it may not seem like a big deal, but to me, it's a sign I've grown, a sign I'm being brave. I've spent years staying home, sticking to a routine, and not trying new things because it was more comfortable sticking with the familiar. Taking this trip to France to surprise Logan is something sixteen-year-old Daphne would have done when she became an adult. I've missed her, and I'm glad she showed up, finally.

"Fingers crossed, Logan likes the renewed version of me I'm becoming," I whisper to myself as we start our descent. My seatmate probably thinks I'm praying. They're not wrong. Part of me worries Logan won't like new me because he's always known cautious, predictable me, and he accepts me that way. I've had enough therapy over the years to know the most important thing is that I love the person I am. Anyone else loving me is a bonus. Intellectually knowing that is one thing. Accepting it in my heart is another. I'm praying my faith in Logan's love isn't misplaced.

I feel the jolt of the landing gear contacting the tarmac and the deceleration of the plane. Someone further back in the cabin applauds. There's always someone who does that. Maybe it's a plant. The pilot welcomes us to Paris and gives the local time and weather while we taxi toward the gate. I unlock my phone to open the text thread and thumb a message to Logan.

> Me: Good morning! Guess where I am?

> Logan: At home in our bed?

> Me: Bzzzzzzz! Wrong answer. Would you like a picture clue?

> Logan: Okay, make sure you're in the picture. I miss your face.

I take a picture out the window to show the jets at the gates next to mine and send it. I'm visible in the reflection on the glass.

> Me: Any guesses?

> Logan: You're on a plane????? Where are you going???

> Me: I'm already there.

> Logan: Sunshine, put me out of my misery. Where are you?

> Me: I don't know the exact gate, but I believe they call it the Charles de Gaulle Airport? Oops, time to get off the plane. I'll FaceTime you once I'm through customs or whatever. I didn't check a bag, so hopefully it won't be too long. See you soon!

I grab my bag from the overhead bin and exit my row to join the slow line of passengers disembarking the plane. I follow the flow of the crowd and let it lead me to where I need to go.

Wow. The massiveness of this space is overwhelming. My eyes jump from the high ceiling to the shops that rival the fanciest of shopping malls. There are people everywhere—babies crying, couples reuniting, business people on their phones making deals. This is so much bigger than I thought it would be. The jostling of the crowd makes me feel like a pebble being carried downstream by a strong current.

My ears are buffeted by conversations in so many languages I don't understand, but the cries of joy when people reunite with their loved ones are universally understood. I smile as I enter the arrival hall where I can meet Logan—if he's in town—and I watch a husband give his wife an enormous bouquet of pale pink roses to welcome her home. I can smell their fragrance from here. Their little boy gives his mother a smaller bouquet of daisies. So sweet. I want to be greeted at the airport by Logan and our children one day. Roses are optional, but hugs are not.

I pull out my phone to message him.

> Me: I'm through everything and in the arrival hall for my terminal. Where do I need to go to meet up with you?

> Logan: Turn around.

I read his message and feel myself doing the confused puppy head tilt he teases me about. I glance up and turn around as directed and find the man I love standing ten feet away. I feel tears gather, at odds with the huge smile spreading across my face. I'm not sure who moved to the other or if we met in the middle, but the next thing I know, I'm enfolded in Logan's embrace, and we're kissing passionately. I've missed this man so much. It's only been three and a half weeks, but it feels like forever.

I almost forget we're in a very public place. Thankfully, I remember in time to stop myself from wrapping my leg around his hips. Public displays of affection are one thing, public displays of fornication are better saved for Amsterdam. With great reluctance, I pull back from our kiss.

"How did you get here so fast?" I ask. My research says it takes at least half an hour to reach the airport on the outskirts of Paris, and it's early in the morning. "Were you already dressed and ready to go?"

Logan grabs my rolling carry-on bag with one hand, takes my hand in the other, and leads me toward a shuttle. "That's a funny story." I think he's blushing. Why is he blushing? "I'm staying at a hotel a few minutes away."

"Why?" I ask. "Isn't it inconvenient to be so far from the city center of Paris? You're wasting a lot of time going back and forth every day."

"If I was traveling back to the city center, it would suck, but if I was catching a flight this afternoon, it's convenient."

Jet lag must be really kicking my ass or I'm extremely dense because I'm not following our conversation.

"I thought you were taking a train to Strasbourg. Are you going somewhere else instead?"

We take our seats aboard the shuttle. I don't know where we're going, but I trust Logan knows what to do.

A horrible thought enters my mind. "Oh no! Am I ruining your plans? I'm sorry!" I feel the sting of tears, and this time, they aren't tears of joy.

"No! You aren't ruining anything, Daph. This is wonderful!" Logan releases my hand so he can wrap his around my shoulder and pull me close for a kiss. This time, we're mindful of our surroundings and keep our kiss to a more PG standard. "I was flying back home to you this afternoon. I was cutting my trip short and coming home."

Wait. What? He was coming home? If I had taken a later flight, I could have arrived after he left, and we'd still be on different continents. My face must telegraph my thoughts because he's quick to reassure me.

"Hey, sunshine. It's okay. We're here together now. I'll change my ticket to fly home with you." He presses a kiss on my forehead. "We're good. When is your flight home scheduled for?"

With a murmured, "Here we are," Logan stands and grasps my hand again to lead me off the shuttle and into another terminal of the airport.

"Where are we?" I follow Logan as we take a covered walkway from the terminal. I don't know if we're going to a parking lot or the train station.

"We're going back to the hotel. It's a couple minutes' walk." He glances back at me.

Wiggling my brows, I try a seductive smile. With my luck, it probably appears like I smelled a fart.

"I want to go to bed, but I'm not tired."

I guess my smile was better than I thought because Logan's gaze flares with a sudden heat. His grip on my hand tightens, and he walks with purpose.

I almost need to jog to keep up with the rapid pace he sets, but I'm not complaining. I'm eager to get to our room too. I'm beyond ready to take our relationship to the next level of intimacy.

Yet, I'm nervous too. I've never been with a man before, but this is Logan. Beyond being my boyfriend, he's my best friend. He'll take care of me and do everything humanly possible to make this a wonderful experience for both of us.

I don't have time to admire the lobby of the modern hotel we enter. Logan leads me to the waiting elevator and hits the button for the third floor. The moment the doors close, he presses me against the side wall of the car and kisses me deeply, his tongue stroking mine in a way that has me pressing my thighs together to relieve the pressure building there. It feels like mere seconds when we arrive at our floor. The doors open, and Logan takes my hand as we exit the elevator.

"Come on, this way," he says, letting go of my hand to slip his arm around my waist. The smooth move propels me to the left so we can walk briskly to a door two-thirds of the way along the hall. Stopping at the door to room 307, Logan waves the card to unlock it and ushers me in.

Straight ahead is a king-size bed with rumpled white sheets. I imagine being in that bed with Logan. The room is small—the bed goes wall-to-wall at the far end of the room, and a TV hangs above it. We essentially walk through the bathroom when we enter the bedroom.

Giving me a grimace tinged with embarrassment, Logan glances around the room as if seeing it for the first time.

"I'm sorry. I was here for the night before flying home. I wasn't expecting you to be here."

I walk further into the room, not that there's very far to go, and sit on the bed. "It's fine. It has a bed and a bathroom. You need little more than that."

He stands but doesn't cross the room to join me on the bed. Why? I pat the mattress—an invitation.

"No way, Daph. I'm not sure I can resist temptation, and I don't want our first time together to be here."

"Logan!" I cry. "I want to be with you. I don't care about the room aesthetics."

Finally, he strides across the room and kneels in front of me. He rests his hands on my jeans-clad knees. "Daphne, I care. I want the first time we make love to be special. I don't want it to be in an airport hotel."

"Are you saying I flew all the way to Paris and I'm not getting boinked?!" I say it in a joking manner, but I'm serious. I missed him, and I'm tired of waiting. I want him. I've been dreaming of being with him for weeks. Does he not want to have sex with me? Has our time apart changed his mind?

Oh no, have I read this situation all wrong? He said he loves me, but he doesn't know I heard him because I didn't tell him I loved him. Is that why he changed his mind? Maybe he wants to go back to being friends? Was there a time limit I wasn't aware of?

"Oh, you're getting boinked today, Daphne," he reassures me, "but not here." He squeezes my knee. "How about this? You take a shower."

I raise my eyebrows in the universally known gesture for *wanna join?*

He chuckles. "Alone. There are limits to my restraint, Daph."

"It's more efficient and environmentally conscious if we shower together, you know," I mention, teasing him.

"Hush, you. I already took my shower, and I know you want to wash the travel cooties off you. I'm running downstairs to grab stuff from the breakfast buffet while you take your shower. No funny business." His earnest gaze meets mine. "Please, Daph. I want to do this right."

Oh, my heart. I couldn't deny this man anything. Leaning forward, I place a quick kiss on his lips because I must. I can't resist him.

"Okay, we will do it your way." I pause. *"This time."* I try out a stern expression to show I'm serious, but I'm uncertain if I pulled it off. "But don't think I'm going to always give in." I squeeze his hands where they rest on my knees. "Now go fetch me food, kind sir. I need to keep my strength up."

After lifting my hand to his lips to place a lingering kiss on the back of it, he stands and gives me a courtly bow. "Yes, milady. Dost thou have any special requests?"

He is such a goof. I tell him to get whatever he thinks is good and watch him walk out the door. I'm sure he's going to dawdle so that I have time to shower and get dressed, but he's right. I want to wash the travel cooties off me. I strip and turn on the shower, adjusting the temperature to something less than scalding. I quickly soap up and rinse off. Using the same soap Logan did feels intimate. Considering what I hope we do tonight, it feels silly to think about the intimacy of using the same bar of soap, but I can't help it. I use the shampoo the hotel supplies because I didn't want to go digging in my bag for the travel-size bottle of my usual shampoo. It smells nice. I feel fancy using French toiletries. I laugh at the sheltered life I've led. By the time Logan returns with a tray holding muffins, bottled water, yogurt, berries, and granola, I'm dressed and running a towel over my hair.

Setting the tray on the small desktop, Logan smiles at me. "Feel better?"

"I do. I'm ready to go on an adventure!" I hug him. I'm in France. With Logan. I can barely believe it! "What are we doing first? I want to do everything!"

"Well, first we're eating breakfast, but while we're doing that, we can figure out what we're going to do next. We can stay in Paris. Or we can take the train to Strasbourg and do the Christmas Market there." He pulls the top off his cinnamon strudel muffin and sets it on my plate. He really loves me; muffin tops are my favorite. "Strasbourg is really neat. It's in the Alsace region of France. There's a long history of French and German culture. Remember, we studied the Cathédrale Notre Dame de Strasbourg in class?"

I can't hold back my happy moan while chewing the bite of muffin. The sweet and spicy flavors are exploding on my tongue.

Logan's eyes darken with my moan. He wants me.

So why is he reluctant to sleep with me? Is it really just that this room isn't that romantic, or is there more to it? Doing my best to push any negative thoughts away, I do an excited Tigger bounce in my chair at the thought of finally seeing in person something I've daydreamed about exploring. That I get to experience it with Logan is a dream come true. We would have lunch after our history and architecture class and talk about the places we wanted to visit, but I never dreamed it would happen for me at all, let alone with Logan by my side as my boyfriend.

I swallow the muffin bite and take a sip of water. "I remember. Let's go to Strasbourg for at least a couple of days. I scheduled my flight home for next Saturday. I'm supposed to be back in the office a week from Monday. Will you be able to change your flight?"

With an overconfident grin splitting his face, he replies, "Sunshine, just wait and see what I can do."

I can't wait. That's part of my frustration! However, I'll channel my inner grown-up, try to be patient, and let Logan plan things how he wishes them to be. This time.

32
LOGAN

While we eat our breakfast, I make train reservations to take us to Strasbourg this afternoon, rent us a room for the next few nights at a hotel I think Daphne will adore, and change my flight to match her return flight next Saturday. I already packed in anticipation of flying home today. Seeing how Daphne never unpacked, it's a simple matter to check out of the room and travel to the rail terminal to take the train to Strasbourg.

"So, tell me about your tours. The Batsto one was neat." It's a two-hour ride, and we spend it holding hands, exchanging kisses, and talking about the tours Daphne has been recording and uploading.

Besides the first tour she posted at the wildlife refuge, she did a second tour at Batsto Village, an abandoned former ironworks town in the middle of Wharton State Forest, now a New Jersey State Historic Site.

"I went there once as a boy but didn't really appreciate it. Watching your video, I saw so many things I wanted to shoot. I'd like to do a seasons series where we visit throughout the year and I take pictures of the same things and see how they change, or don't change, in a year's time. I've never done something like that."

I haven't done it since I'm never in the same place long-term. I'm surprised at how excited I am. I'm also slightly shocked because I knew I would be excited to be with Daphne, but I was expecting to feel like I was sacrificing to be with her. Suddenly, I'm seeing opportunities, and being home isn't a sacrifice. It's so exciting to explore and discover things I've taken for granted. Being with Daphne is the impetus for returning home, but I'm also realizing the wonderful things about a place I've always been so eager to leave. Can you fall in love with a place the same way you do a person?

"Let's grab a taxi to take us to the hotel," I say as we exit the train in Strasbourg.

Daphne reads the clock on the wall of the station. "Isn't it too early to check in?"

"I arranged for our bags to be held at reception so we could get lunch and walk around. They'll bring them to our room when it's ready, so we simply need to get our key from reception when we come back. Nothing to it."

"You've thought this through. Impressive, Mr. Morris." She says it teasingly, but I intend on impressing the socks—and panties—off Miss Foster tonight.

I hail a cab and ask the driver to take us to our hotel. Daphne's gasp of delight when we pull up confirms I made the right choice. The centuries-old hotel is a charming hodgepodge of French and German architectural styles with timber trim on the exterior, wooden balconies and walkways, wrought-iron gates, and leaded glass windows. A porter takes our bags and escorts us into the hotel.

"Logan, so nice to see you again! And you must be the lovely Daphne—welcome!" My friend Luc waits for us at the reception desk and greets me with a hearty handshake and a kiss for each of Daphne's cheeks. He's the general manager and kindly agreed to do me this favor based on our years of friendship. We originally met in Austria and spent a few months traveling Europe together, drinking lots of beer and being crazy. He knows all about Daphne and was happy to hear that I finally got my act together enough to have a romantic relationship with her. When I messaged to see if there was a room available for the next few days, and if we could do a few things to make our stay special, he was happy to help. He's a romantic at heart.

I can see Daphne's confusion, so I explain. "Luc is the general manager here. I've told you about him." I see her make the connection and the genuine smile spread across her face.

"Luc!" She gives him a hug and presses a kiss to his cheek. "It's so wonderful to meet you! How's Bernard?"

"Bernard's doing well. He's traveling to open a new restaurant this week. He'll be so disappointed not to meet you."

The valet stashed our bags in a room behind the reception area, and I slip him a tip with a smile.

"Do you want to be texted when your room is ready, or will you be out until later?" Luc asks.

Daphne shrugs.

I study her a moment. Her gaze is alert, and her movements are full of energy. She's ready to go exploring and see everything she's only read about, but jet lag is going to body-check her against the boards at some point.

Grinning, she pats my shoulder. "Stop worrying! I'm good for at least another few hours. I'm finally here in France and want to go exploring! No sleeping until bedtime." She winks, the flirty gleam in her eyes telling me that while she's not sleeping until bedtime, there's another way I can get her into bed earlier. I'm all for that, but we need to stretch the time until we can go to our room.

"We'll come back after check-in time, Luc. Thanks." I take Daph's hand, and we say goodbye to Luc and leave the hotel. "What do you want for lunch? I think room service may be our best choice for dinner tonight, if that's okay with you."

"Don't laugh at me over this. Yes, we're in France and there are all kinds of wonderful foods, but I'm craving pub grub. I want comfort food."

I'm not surprised to hear this from her. She's been this way since I've known her. When she's tired, all she wants are her favorite foods before she crawls into bed, dead to the world.

I think of the perfect thing. "I figured you would. There's an Irish pub near here. Feel up to walking? It's across the bridge, about a five-minute walk." It's cool but not cold, so walking won't be too uncomfortable, and we can see a bit of the neighborhood on the way.

She nods eagerly. "That sounds perfect! Let's go."

Hand in hand, we walk along the century-old streets and cross the bridge over the River Ill. We marvel at the buildings and admire our fellow pedestrians. It's easy to spot the tourists walking among the locals by the way they point at the buildings and stop to admire a view. Daphne and I are guilty of the same things.

We discuss topics we covered in our history and architecture class where we first met, and it reminds me of how we initially became friends. I thought she was pretty and found her attractive, but then we became friends, and that friendship has grown into so much more through the years. I can't believe we're here, walking these streets together, her hand in mine.

My heart is hers, and we're finally going to be together fully.

I've never been this nervous about sleeping with a woman, not even when I was a virgin. This is the first time I've been in love with the woman I'm sleeping with. We won't only be having sex, we'll make love. It's intimidating.

Of course, I've always been respectful of my partner. They always knew going into an encounter it wasn't love. It was satisfying mutual needs, and I made damn sure I always satisfied their needs before satisfying mine.

But I want this to be wonderful for Daphne. After all, it's her first time, not just with me, but at all. Part of me wants to drag her back to our room and love her like I've been longing to. Another part of me wants to keep walking, holding her hand, talking, laughing, and enjoying each other's company without the pressure of sex.

"Is this it?" Daphne asks when we approach the Irish pub.

I nod, and we approach the entrance. Painted on the wall next to the door are historic notes about the building. Daphne knows Spanish, so she understands the general idea of what the French text means because of similarities in the two languages, but I want to show off and translate it for her.

"That's the first time I've heard you speak French," she says. "It's very sexy." She stretches to kiss me.

Wrapping my arms around her, I whisper French terms of endearment in her ear along with a few nonsense phrases about my car needing an oil change and sheep playing baseball on the moon. She emits the cutest giggle when I nuzzle the spot under her ear where I discovered she's ticklish.

Pulling away, she grabs my hand and opens the door before I have the chance to be a gentleman and open it for her.

"I appreciate you're an independent person, Daph, but I enjoy taking care of you sometimes," I grumble.

She laughs. "If I stood around waiting for someone to open a door for me, I'd get nowhere." She tugs me further inside.

She's not wrong. I'll have to find other ways to take care of her. Looking forward to it. We sit at a table and, after reading the menu, decide we each want the Irish stew and a pint of Guinness.

Laughing, I share that I had gone years without eating stew and now it seems to be a meal I eat all the time. First at Uncle Will and Aunt Faith's, then with Mari's family, and now today with her.

"I know!" she exclaims. "Maybe it's a trend or the time of year because it seems like it is everywhere. Is stew the new chili?"

"Here you go," our server says in accented English as he places our bowls of stew and a basket of hearty bread on our table. "Do you need anything else?"

"We're good, thank you," I reply.

"Merci." Daphne smiles up at him. I swear he melts a little. It's the Daphne Effect. She has a way of charming people, and she's unaware of it. It's another item on the miles-long list of things I love and appreciate about her.

"Oh my goodness, this is delicious!" Daphne appears to be near rapture with her first spoonful of stew. The rich scent of lamb, carrots, onions, and potatoes has my mouth watering. Paired with the Guinness, it almost feels like we are sitting in a pub in Ireland. I can't wait to take her there for the authentic experience.

"We need to do a taste test," I say, "and compare this stew with actual Irish stew eaten in a pub on Irish soil." I reach out and grasp her hand resting on the table. "There are so many places I want to show you and fresh places I want to explore for the first time with you. I hope this week is the first of many adventures together." I lift her hand to press a gentle kiss to her knuckles and then lower it back to the table before picking up my spoon and taking my next taste of the stew.

"I would love to go to Ireland with you, Logan. I want to go everywhere with you." She smiles at me across the table.

Those are the words I've waited years to hear from Daphne. But does she really mean them? I've made peace with not traveling as much and setting up a business to take advantage of what we have at home. I'm looking forward to implementing my idea. I think it's something unique.

Oblivious to my thoughts, Daphne sips her Guinness and pushes away her bowl. "I want to eat all of this, but I'm going to fall into a food coma if I do. Can we come back here later in the week for another bowl? Now that I know what to expect, I can be sure to breakfast responsibly so there's plenty of room, and we can walk after to help burn it off."

"That sounds like a good plan, Daph. Are you sure you're done?" I'm sopping up the last of my stew with a piece of bread.

"You're totally going to scavenge my leftovers, aren't you?" She doesn't even sound surprised.

She shouldn't be. I've done this to her many times. "There's no point in letting this delicious food go to waste. Besides, I need to keep my strength up." I waggle my brows.

She blushes a deep rose, and I love it. She goes seagull swooping in on my French fries all the time, so I don't feel the least bit guilty switching our bowls to take her remaining stew and leaving my empty bowl in front of her.

"Anyway," I add, "if we're coming back here, we don't want to insult the chef by not emptying our bowls. What if they decide we aren't worthy and won't serve us? I'm doing this for us, sunshine."

With a grin, she says, "That's you, Logan Morris, taking one for the team. What a hero."

I polish off the remaining stew and pay the bill when the server presents it. It's almost check-in time at the hotel, so we walk back at a leisurely pace.

I spy a pharmacy and lead us toward it. "Um, I need to run in here." I can feel a slight flush heat my cheeks. I'm a twenty-six-year-old man that has been having sex for over a decade. Buying condoms is not an unfamiliar experience for me. I should not be blushing.

"Okay. For what?" Daphne asks, following me in.

Condom shopping is not a group activity, so I stop in front of the door. My face grows hotter. This is ridiculous. "I need to get a box of condoms." My face must be scarlet.

"Why?"

Seriously, what's with the questions? An older gentleman is approaching behind Daphne, so I clasp her elbow to lead her to the side.

"Because I don't have any with me. I wasn't having sex on this trip, so there was no reason to pack condoms. I'm hoping we're sleeping together sometime soon, so I want to be prepared." I break off when a mother with her young daughter exits the shop and glances over at us.

"Oh, that makes sense," Daphne replies. "I brought a box with me though. I checked to see what you had in the dresser of your old room and bought a fresh box of the same kind. I hope you still like them. The box you had expired a couple of years ago."

The older gentleman is now exiting the store.

"I got some lube too, just in case. I'm on the pill now and have been for a few weeks, so it should be effective, but I'd feel more comfortable if we use condoms, at least until after my next period."

I don't know why the thought of Daphne taking charge and buying condoms both turns me on and shocks me, but it does. Of course, we're equally responsible for contraception, but I thought she'd be too shy to buy condoms. I felt a little awkward the first time I picked up tampons for her. It's just so...personal.

"All righty, then," I say, grasping her hand and leading us away from the shop.

This is happening. Finally. I've wanted her for years but thought the most we'd ever be was friends. These past few weeks...knowing we're so much more than best friends but not yet lovers...have been torturous. My heart rate speeds up as we approach the doors of the hotel, and I send up a silent prayer. Oh, Lord, please don't let me have a heart attack before I make love to this beautiful woman. Amen.

As we enter the lobby, someone calls out, "Monsieur Morris, Mademoiselle Foster?"

We turn and nod.

A gorgeous dark-skinned woman bustles toward us, a brilliant smile gracing her pretty face. "Your room is ready, and your luggage is upstairs. Mr. Girard asked to be informed if there was anything you need. Please ask if there is something we can do to make your stay with us more comfortable."

I accept the room keys from her outstretched hand and thank her.

Squeezing my hand, Daphne smiles up at me. "Ready to go upstairs?" At my nod, she leads the way upstairs. When we reach our room, I open the door and step aside for her to enter first.

"Oh my, this is beautiful!" Daphne exclaims, turning a slow circle in the center of the room. The whitewashed walls stand in stark contrast to the heavy timber beams that adorn them. My glance falls on the large double bed dressed in white linens.

"Ooh! There's a clawfoot tub!" Daphne calls out from the bathroom.

I wander over to check it out.

"It looks big enough for two," she says with a grin and a waggle of her brows.

I grin back. "Do you need a bath, Daphne? Are you a dirty girl?" Holy crap, I can't believe I said that.

Her bark of laughter signals she wasn't expecting me to say something so cheesy, either. She's still laughing, and now I'm a tad concerned she's going to suffer from a reduced oxygen supply.

"Oh, my God, Logan... has that line actually worked for you?" She wipes tears from her eyes.

I chuckle, feeling sheepish. "I've never used that line before."

"Yay, I'm your first!"

I go still. She's teasing me. I can hear that in her voice, but I can see a flash of insecurity on her face. Damn.

I motion to the seating area. "Come on, let's talk."

"Do we have to?" Daphne whines.

I march into the sitting area and sit tall on the couch, not even stopping to hear her arguments. I cross my arms over my chest and stare steadily at her. "Yes, we have to."

She flops in the armchair with all the grace of a rag doll. "What?"

"Does it bother you that I have a past? That you aren't the first person I've slept with?" This is the last conversation I want to be having right now, but it's an important conversation we need to have.

"No. You'd slept with women before you ever knew I existed. You've slept with women since we've known each other. What matters to me is that you don't sleep with anyone other than me while we're together."

I'm offended. "Daphne, I've never been a cheater. You're the only woman I want to be with. There won't be anyone else. There hasn't been anyone else for years. Once I realized I wasn't getting you out of my system, there was no point. I love you."

Tears spring to her eyes, and she raises a hand to cover her heart. "Oh, Logan, I love you too. I've always loved you. You're all that I've ever wanted."

Wow. This is real. I'm not surprised. I knew how I felt. I thought I knew how Daphne felt. But it's happening. Is it possible for your world to shift on its axis and also right itself in the same moment? The smile spreading across Daphne's face must mirror mine. I guess it is possible.

She places a hand on my thigh and gives a light squeeze. My cock responds by hardening. She notices and moves her hand toward it. I place my hand on hers to stop the migration.

She looks at me quizzically. "Are you okay?"

"Yeah, I'm fine, just not sure how to do this." Crap. Why did I say that?

"How to do what? How to sleep together?" She tilts her head. "You have done this before, right? You're not secretly a virgin too, are you?"

"We've established I'm not a virgin." I chuckle. "But this is your first time, so I want it to be good for you." I lift her hand from my thigh and kiss her palm. "I want it to be good for us. I love you."

Getting up and climbing into my lap, Daphne clasps my jawline with her hands and kisses me. It's not a passionate kiss. Rather, it's a kiss of love and trust. It's the kiss of a lover reassuring her partner that she wants this. I don't know how long we sit there kissing. It could be five minutes, or it could be an hour, but eventually, kissing isn't enough for either of us. I stand from my chair, lifting Daphne in my arms.

She breaks our kiss to give a startled, "Oh!"

When she realizes I'm headed to our bed, her next "Oh" is more of a sigh. I place a knee on the mattress so I can lower her gently to the surface of the bed. Her arms around my neck pull me down with her, and our kisses and caresses continue. I can't believe I'm finally going to make love to the woman I cherish, to my best friend, to my forever.

33
DAPHNE

"WHEN THEY SAID HAVING SEX THE FIRST TIME COULD BE PAINFUL FOR women, I thought they meant physically. I didn't realize they meant painfully awkward." I roll my head on the pillow to glance over at Logan coming in from the bathroom, having disposed of the condom and cleaned up. His chest is heaving, his hair tousled.

He climbs back in our bed with a laugh. "It would't have been so awkward if you hadn't mooed!"

My laughter bursts forth. "I'm sorry! When you were sucking on my nipple, it felt so good. Then I got thinking of the time we were at that farm. The calf latched on to nurse, and the mommy cow let out a surprised '*Mooooo!*'—I couldn't help it." I roll to my side and snuggle up, resting my head on his chest and feeling his arms encircle me. "I admire and appreciate your ability to focus and get the job done, even with my silliness."

He leans down and kisses me. "Next time I'm going to make you so crazy you won't think of anything but me."

I run my hand down his torso and fondle his cock. "So, what you're saying is I shouldn't cry out for you to give me your cock-a-doodle-doo while I'm in the throes of passion?"

His chest is making my head bounce from how hard he's laughing.

"Oh my God, Daphne, don't you dare! I'm afraid it will quickly become a cock-a-doodle-don't."

I squeeze his cock that is hardening in my grasp and search Logan's face. "How long before it's a cock-a-doodle-let's-do-it-again?"

Rolling me onto my back, he kisses me deeply. "I didn't think of you as the insatiable type."

"It's your fault for being so good at this." I can't suppress my moan as he kisses down my neck and across my collarbone. This time, when he takes my nipple in his mouth, I arch my back and beg for more. He keeps his promise. I'm so focused on him, I can't think of farms we visited or funny jokes or anything other than his body making love to mine. All this glorious skin—every last inch, even the parts that aren't twelve inches but are totally wonderful however many inches they are—stretched over his muscular body is available for me to touch. There is no awkwardness. We're both quick learners. I discover running my nails from the nape of his neck and through his hair, massaging his scalp, causes him to shiver and let out a low moan that does *things* to me. It's not just the moan, it's the way his fingers skim down my side and skate past my belly button to my clit. He knows the perfect motions and just the right amount of pressure to bring me to the edge. As he eases his cock into me, stretching me, filling me, his lips move from my breast, across my collarbone, up my throat, raining little kisses, little nips, and soothing licks on his way to kiss me. His mouth is firm but gentle against mine, his tongue caressing. I grab his ass and try to flex my hips against him to get him to start moving. I know why he's being slow and gentle, I'm new at this, but I want it all. So what if I'm sore or walk funny for a day or two? I packed Tylenol and I'm a tourist. No matter what I do, I'll be met with a certain amount of French disdain. When Logan breaks our kiss to bury his head where my shoulder and neck meet, I lean my head to give him more access.

"Logan, more," I pant. "I love you, give me more. It's okay. Love me."

That's all that needed to be said for Logan to give a low, sexy growl, move his hands to my hips to anchor me, and start moving harder and faster. His thrusts are deep and rhythmic and hitting spots I didn't realize needed hitting. My breath comes faster, and I feel my release bearing down on me. I've had orgasms before, I know how to pleasure myself, but to have them with someone...with Logan...is everything. I cry out as my orgasm hits and I tighten around him, his thrusts become more staccato as he comes too, shuddering as his release pulses through him. His weight is heavy on me, but I love it. If we could stay like this forever, I'd have everything I've ever wanted.

I've missed waking in Logan's arms. Not that we slept much last night, but the sleep we got was restful. I don't want to leave the warm cocoon of our bed.

Logan reaches out and runs a finger along my cheek, his gaze tender. "I love you."

I will never tire of hearing those words. "I know. I'm irresistible."

Jumping up to avoid being tickled by his questing fingers, I throw over my shoulder, "I love you too. Now get your fine ass out of bed and get ready."

We already showered after our last lovemaking session, so we're presentable with a minimum of fuss, thank goodness. I'm starving. We had room service sandwiches last night for a late dinner, but our activities worked up quite an appetite in me, and not solely for food. But food is the most pressing need.

The continental breakfast served in the hotel's dining room was delightful, but I'm famished for lunch after walking all morning to the Cathédrale Notre Dame de Strasbourg and then touring the magnificent Gothic cathedral. It was breathtaking. I'm awestruck by all the history here. Toto, I'm not in South Jersey anymore.

After lunch at a café, we stroll back to our hotel. I'm still jet-lagged, and neither of us got a full night of sleep. We decide a nap before dinner is what we need. Dinner ends up being room service again.

Oops. Not sorry.

"I have a surprise for you," Logan whispers in my ear to wake me the next morning.

"Again? Are there still condoms left?" It's too early for me to do mental math, but I think we're close to running out.

Chuckling, he nuzzles that spot that makes me giggle and causes me to squirm. "We need to pick up more while we're out. But first, I've arranged for us to be given a private tour of the hotel."

He presses a kiss to my neck, and I hope the tour isn't soon. That dream is dashed when he rolls away and gets out of bed. I appreciate the view of his gorgeous body, but I wish it was still here in bed with me.

"Time to rise and shine, sunshine—breakfast, tour, and then Christmas markets. I know I've turned you into a sex fiend, but we can't spend all our time in here boinking. We need to experience this beautiful town."

"Logan," I whine, "come back to bed. I miss you!"

It doesn't work because that fine ass walks into the bathroom and closes the door. Ugh. When the door opens a few moments later, I think I'm going to get my way, but no. Logan is being a gentleman, asking if I need to use the bathroom before he gets in the shower. We may be best friends and lovers, but our relationship is most definitely not at the *let's pee in front of each other* stage. We should save some things for after marriage...or for never.

I start the shower in hopes Logan will join me. Like always, he doesn't disappoint me. Many soapy minutes later leave neither of us disappointed—getting clean has never felt so dirty. Rising from my knees, I finish rinsing off and step out of the shower into the warm towel Logan is holding open for me.

"Daphne, these have been the best days of my life. I love you so much," he tells me while he folds me in the towel.

I wrap my arms around him and rest my head against his chest. Hearing his heartbeat is one of my most favorite sounds in the entire world. I place a kiss on his pec and melt a bit when he kisses the crown of my head. I love hair kisses. I never knew that was a thing for me, but coming from Logan, it is. Okay, kisses anywhere coming from Logan do it for me, but the gentleness and affection of those kisses make my tummy flip.

"C'mon, we need to dress so we can have breakfast and do our tour. Lots of things to do today," he says, securing my towel and pulling away. He hands me a second towel so I can run it over my dripping hair. The towel wrapped around his trim waist drops to the floor when he turns to walk into the bedroom. I enjoy the view before moving to the bathroom counter to get ready.

34
LOGAN

THE PRIVATE TOUR OF THE HOTEL IS CAPTIVATING. THE GUIDE SHARES SO much information about the history of the property and the unique architectural features, like a well dating back to the sixteenth century and stunning stained-glass windows.

The tour guide ambles ahead and turns the corner. Before Daphne can follow, I pull her against me and press my lips to hers, this hallway the spotlight for our love story, with the dappled winter sunlight coming through the leaded windows.

"We could spend a month here taking tours and never be bored. I love doing things like this with you." I rub my nose against hers. "Enjoying our nerdy hobbies. Having fun."

Being lovers is wonderful, but first and foremost, she's my best friend, and I've missed being with her like this. As much as I'd love to spend a month here with her, I'm also eager to go home. I'm ready to start our life together and implement the ideas I have for my career. But she's so excited, loving every minute of our adventure. I don't know how to bring up changing our plans and flying home early. This is her first trip. I don't want to cheat her out of the experience.

"If we buy things at the markets," Daphne says as we approach the first Christmas Market, "how are we getting them home?"

She swings our clasped hands back and forth while we walk. It's adorable. Liam would tease me for being a sappy wuss, but I don't care. There will come a day when he falls in love and will do sappy, wussy things, and I'll be happy for him. I'll also rag on him because that's what we do, but I'll still be happy for him.

Squeezing her hand, I swing along with her. "I guess it depends how much we buy. The easiest thing to do would be to pack things in our bags. We can move things around to make room. Or we could buy a bag and check it if necessary. You had the carry-on, so another bag isn't a big deal. We'll figure it out."

"Cool. I want to pick up something for Mallory as a souvenir and then something else for her Christmas gift. Maybe we can find Christmas presents for your family?"

She gasps.

We've hit our first glimpse of the Place Gutenberg market, and she's all wide eyes and open mouth.

I smile. Christmas markets here aren't like the festivals and craft shows at home with the rows of white pop-up tents. Here, vendors build wooden stalls and there are festive lights strung overhead. It's magical. Fortunately, it's not bitterly cold and uncomfortable to be outside, but it's still cold enough that Daphne snuggles against my side for warmth. The day is overcast, so the lights are lit this afternoon.

"It's like being in a Hallmark movie," Daphne breathes. I bark out a laugh because that's such a random thing to say, but it's true.

"If this was a Hallmark movie, there would be a wise shopkeeper sharing the secret of Christmas with someone who lost sight of the true meaning of the holiday. There would be snowflakes. Oh, and a horse-drawn carriage ride."

Laughing, Daphne rests her head against my arm before stretching to press a kiss on my cheek.

"And if it was a Howlbark movie, the horses would end up being shifters earning extra money to save their family's farm." She takes a deep breath and groans. "Let's grab a snack. Everything smells so good!"

She leads me to a stall full of baked goods where we decide to get one pretzel topped with chocolate and a second more traditional savory version with salt and share both. We'll stop for dinner on the way back to the hotel, so the pretzels—they call them bretzels here, but it's a pretzel as far as we're concerned—are a nice snack to hold the worst of our hunger at bay.

Daphne moans when she takes a bite of the salted pretzel. "Oh my gosh. This is so good."

I've heard that moan several times this weekend, and my cock doesn't care that it's in a different context. He still stirs in interest. How he wasn't hard every time he was within six feet of Daphne through the years, I don't know. Not that he had much of an opportunity. It's part of the reason I traveled so much. It was pure torture to be near Daphne when I thought I couldn't be with her the way I longed to be. Now that she's mine, I don't plan on traveling as much, especially if she can't come with me.

As we wander the assorted markets, I get great shots of the stalls and the decorations. It's merely a coincidence that Daphne is often in the frame.

"Why do you keep taking pictures of me? There are all these wonderful things here. You don't need to be taking pictures of me."

Oops.

"Well, I was going through my portfolio, I was surprised to see how few pictures of you I had. Of course, most of my photos are from my travels, but I realized that when I'm home, I rarely have my camera in hand. I spend my time with you doing things and not looking at them through a lens."

We browse through the stalls and select a bunch of items to give as gifts for Christmas. We find earrings for the ladies in my family and Mallory. And while Daphne hovers around another stall considering mugs for the guys, I find a pair of heart-shaped amber earrings and buy them. The shade reminds me of the color of Daphne's eyes after we've made love, and I want her to have them. As a souvenir for Mallory, we select a figurine of a timber-trimmed building like the ones surrounding us. You put a small candle or bulb inside to illuminate it. It's neat and reminds me of something.

"Are these the right scale for the Christmas village you have?" I ask. "Or are they too small?" I haven't seen the display in years because I haven't been home at Christmas since we graduated college. I don't remember how big the ceramic houses are that Daphne and her gran used to set up in the bay window as a charming holiday decoration.

Tilting her head to consider them, Daphne answers, "I think they're too small. To be honest, I haven't seen them in years, so I don't know."

"What do you mean, you haven't seen them in years? Where are they?" I'm dreading the answer I think I'm going to get.

"Packed away." She shrugs. "I haven't decorated in years. There didn't seem to be a point when I'm the only one seeing them." She picks up a building. It's a church. She examines it for a moment and puts it back on the display. "They decorate the office and the lobby at work, and Mallory has a little tree for our section, so I get to enjoy decorations without having to do any of the work."

Luc recommended that we take shopping bags to carry our purchases, and I'm grateful. I feel like we've bought out the markets between the mugs, ornaments, jewelry, and the house for Mallory. I grab the card from the stall with the houses. I want to see if I can purchase a bunch of them and have them shipped to us as a surprise for Daph.

We decide to take our loot back to the hotel before having dinner. I'm determined to have something other than room service sandwiches tonight.

"That's cheating!" Daphne cries when I give our bags and a hefty tip to a valet to take them to our room.

"No, it's being strategic," I reply. "If we're going to the pub for dinner, we need to do that before we're in the room." I wink. "We can stop by the pharmacy on the way back and pick up anything we need."

Daphne peers at me with an excited expression. "Like candy bars?" With a sheepish expression, she admits, "Even though this is France and there are all these fancy things, I really want to try some of the weird, mass-produced, buy-it-off-the-shelf candy." This is my girl—offer her lobsters and filet mignon, and she's going to crave a cheeseburger. I love her.

Laughing, I admit, "I was planning on buying more condoms, but if candy bars are what make you happy, we'll get them too."

We hold hands as we walk through the early evening. This is our first time being out in Strasbourg after dark. Previously, by the time darkness fell, we'd locked ourselves in our room, enjoying each other's bodies until we fell asleep, sated.

Strolling the historic streets under the cover of night with Daphne is romantic, and I feel fanciful imagining how many other lovers have walked these same streets through the ages. That's one thing I love most about Europe, the sense of history. Of course, other places throughout the world have places with buildings and towns older than these French streets, but they don't resonate with me the same way these old European cities do. I love the cobblestones and narrow roadways, timber beams, and thatched roofs. It all tells a story I'm eager to hear.

The pub is busier than it was the first time we dined here, but we manage to get a table. The TVs are on, with one screen showing a soccer match and another showing rugby. The rugby match isn't featuring teams we follow, so we don't worry about being able to see the screen, but we do glance at it when the patrons groan or cheer depending on the on-field action.

We debate whether to get the stew we loved before or something else from the menu. There are interesting burgers we'd like to try. It's ridiculous to travel to these locales with incredible local cuisine and then get a cheeseburger, but you can learn a lot by seeing how a place does a cheeseburger. They don't always use beef, for example, and they base the rolls on the common bread of the area. The toppings can be extravagant, like foie gras or unusual cheeses, and the portion sizes are often a surprise. In the US, we're used to big burgers that are getting larger with a mountain of fries on the side. In other places, the burgers are smaller and come with a small hill of fries, but the flavors are so incredible you don't even care that you're eating less because it's so satisfying. We could probably do a global burger tour documenting different burgers worldwide. In the end, we decide to do the stew again because it was so good.

After our glasses of red wine arrive, we chat about the Christmas markets and how beautiful the city is at night.

Daphne is fidgety. I reach across and cover her tapping fingers with my hand. "Daph, what's up?"

I can see her weighing her words before she speaks. "I love Strasbourg and being here with you."

I nod, half afraid of what's going to come next. Has she changed her mind about being together after having a taste of what it could be like? Is she going to say she wants to move here? I'd be okay with that, but I can't imagine it being something Daphne wants.

"How upset would you be if we tried to switch our tickets and fly home tomorrow night or Wednesday night so we can have Thanksgiving with your parents?" She appears apprehensive, and while I'm surprised she wants to cut the trip short, I'm touched she wants to spend the holiday with my family.

"Why would I be upset?"

"You plan everything out and get upset when your plan changes," she says.

"Yeah, I'm realizing this unfortunate trait of mine. I'm sorry. I don't mean to be pushy or self-centered. I'm used to only focusing on myself and only being concerned with what I want." I don't mean to be controlling. It's the last thing I want. It makes me feel sick I've unintentionally been that way with Daphne, and I'm determined to change.

"You try to hide it, and I'm not sure you're even aware of it, but you have a plan, and that's the way it is."

"I honestly wasn't aware of it. Everyone always lets me get away with it. Now that I know, I'll work on changing. I trust you'll tell me if I fall back on old habits?"

"Oh, I will," she assures me.

With a sheepish smile, I admit, "I was trying to figure out a way I could ask you about going home for Thanksgiving. I don't want to cut your trip short now that you're finally here, especially since you haven't seen much outside of our room."

Her blushing giggle causes my heart to stutter.

I continue, "I promise we can come back and explore more. I realized I missed home and want to spend our first holiday together as a couple with our family, and they are *our* family. You're one of us. You aren't alone. You're never going to be alone."

I wish I was a painter so I could capture the glowing smile that spreads across her face at my statement on canvas. I'm not, so it will just have to live as a memory tattooed on my heart. Daphne leans across the table and the bustle of the pub fades away as she places a fun kiss on the tip of my nose. As she settles back in her seat, her fingers lace with mine, just like our lives are entwining. "I know."

And I know that, New Jersey or France, bar grub or fine dining, we will always be together. Forever.

EPILOGUE

DAPHNE

"Phew, 199 steps later, we're at the top of the Cape May Lighthouse! You don't want to skip leg day preparing to do this one."

I traverse the walkway around the top of the lighthouse and observe the stunning vista.

"Check out this view, adventurers! You can see the Atlantic Ocean over there. Below us on the beach is a bunker from World War II, built to help protect the coast and stop enemy forces if they tried to land here. That cement structure there in the distance is the World War II Lookout Tower."

Continuing my way around, I exclaim, "Ooh, you can see the Cape May Ferry starting its journey across the Delaware Bay to Lewes, Delaware. That will be a future adventure for us!"

I had an enthusiastic response to the first tours I posted in the fall, so I fulfilled my dream of being a tour guide and worked with Logan to create a blog and YouTube channel showcasing tourist attractions and other scenic adventures. I wear a video camera so our viewers can see what I see while I tell the stories of the places we are visiting, and Logan takes still pictures to post on our blog. He also sells the prints as artwork or has the images available to print on other items. He started his photo tourism business and has hosted a couple of groups so far, taking them to the wildlife refuge to give them tips on photographing wildlife and dealing with technical aspects like light reflection on water. We are planning other trips to Batsto and Cape May in the coming months.

Today I was finally brave enough to climb my first lighthouse. No lie, I'm scared of being this high up. I went up in front, partially so I couldn't chicken out and sneak back down the stairs, but mostly so the view I was recording wasn't Logan's butt all the way up.

No way am I sharing that view. It's all mine.

We've been dating for a few months, and it's been wonderful. We live together in Gran's house—our house—and it is our home base between adventures. I moved to the marketing department at Morgan Development with one of my duties being to create content that shows off the retail centers Morgan has around the country, along with things to see and do in the area. The goal is to attract shoppers to the stores and tie into the local tourism. There's been cross-promotion with the local attractions, so everyone wins.

Logan and I work as a team. He handles the still photography and video while I do the narration and on-camera work. While we're traveling for Morgan, we've been recording adventures for our site, adding a new one every month. Thanks to advice and reposts from Shelby, our following is growing, and we're attracting sponsors other than Morgan Development. Logan wants to expand his photo tourism business to include tours in the places we travel to for work. We have so many ideas, and it's exciting that we've worked out a way to do it together.

After I finish my circuit around the top of the tower, sharing the sights, I turn around to see Logan behind me on one knee.

Oh my goodness.

In his hand is a small dark blue velvet box.

He gazes up at me lovingly. "Daphne, being with you has been a wonderful adventure, and I hope to have many more years and countless adventures with you. I love you. Will you please marry me?"

I pull him to his feet and throw my arms around him. "Yes! Of course, I'll marry you!"

I kiss him with happy tears streaming down my face. "I love you, Logan Morris, and by your side is where I want to be. Forever. Now show me that ring!" I say, laughing.

He opens the box, and there are two rings inside—my mother's original Cape May diamond engagement ring Dad gave her, and a beautiful diamond solitaire in a platinum setting.

Logan clears his throat. "I brought your mom's ring so that they're here with us too. I wish I had known them. I would have loved them."

He slips the solitaire on my finger and whispers, "Forever."

"Forever," I echo.

When we descend the lighthouse steps, I'm surprised that it's more nerve-racking than climbing up because I can see how far the fall would be. Logan leads me to the bench we sat on last fall on the day we admitted we wanted to be more than just friends. There is now a plaque on it that has today's date and the words "Logan and Daphne Morris—he asked, she said yes."

I turn to him. "You were that certain I'd say yes? Cocky, aren't you?"

With a wink, he replies, "That's what you were saying last night, and it wasn't a complaint."

Did you enjoy Daphne and Logan's story? Want a peek into their future? Get a bonus scene by subscribing to my mailing list at this link. https://dl.bookfunnel.com/bf75ltelql

ALSO BY JENNY FENSHAW

PARANORMAL HOCKEY LEAGUE

Sexy Pucking Polar Bear

Secret Pucking Unicorn

Flirty Pucking Wolf

Bashful Pucking Bigfoot

SHIFTING PINES - SMALL TOWN SHIFTER ROMANCE

Claiming Her Cougar

MONSTER BRIDES

Bigfoot Finds A Bride

KEEP IN TOUCH!

Follow Jenny now for her romantic stories, stay for her ridiculous personality.

Warning: Snort laughing possible.

If you'd like to keep in touch with Jenny Fenshaw check out Jenny's website for all the ways to connect

https://jennyfenshaw.com/
Or just scan the QR code!

ABOUT THE AUTHOR

Jenny Fenshaw is a funny, goofy, and creative author of contemporary paranormal romantic comedies who loves daydreaming about ordinary events, making them ridiculous, and including them in her stories. A native of southern New Jersey, Jenny loves to set her stories in the area she knows so well. From the Atlantic City Boardwalk to the Pine Barrens, her stories are a love letter to her hometown just as much as they are the love story of her characters.

When she's not writing, Jenny enjoys watching ice hockey (for research!) and reruns of *Murder, She Wrote*. She has been married to her cinnamon roll of a husband for over thirty years and has a grown son who has the best adventures.

f facebook.com/JennyFenshawAuthor

instagram.com/jennyfenshawauthor

BB bookbub.com/authors/jenny-fenshaw

www.ingramcontent.com/pod-product-compliance
Lightning Source LLC
Chambersburg PA
CBHW021927240626
47158CB00001B/2

* 9 7 8 1 9 6 2 6 1 5 0 9 9 *